CENTRAL LINE

CENTRAL LINE

BOOK ONE OF THE CENTRAL LINE TRILOGY

KIARA J. MCKENZIE

Central Line

First Edition: December 2020
Published by: Finch's Whisper Publishing

This is a work of fiction. Names, characters, places, events and incidents either are a product of the author's imagination or are used fictitiously. Any resemblance to actual persons, living or dead, events, or locales is purely coincidental.

Paperback ISBN: 978-1-7771947-0-3
eBook ISBN: 978-1-7771947-1-0

Edited by: Emerald Ink Publishing
Formatting by: Julia Scott (Evenstar Books)
Cover Design by: Hampton Lamoureux (TS95Studios)

To Pepper.

PROLOGUE

"GOOD EVENING, GENERAL SALICES." Though my father's voice radiated chauvinistic confidence when he spoke, I recognized the spike of wryness to his tone. His usual grin—meant to charm those who played into his hands—tugged at his lips, still smooth with the remnants of his youth. Running his hands over his chest, he flattened the material of his blazer. Each move was calculated, submitting to an unknown force. Standing next to him, more aware of my proximity to him than before he'd opened the door, I straightened my shoulders and held my breath.

"One's appearance is the universal key to any door of opportunity otherwise locked," my father had once said to me. And the words needed no reminder, because the night they'd first *graced* my ears, Murus—my father—had struck me, knocking one of my baby teeth loose and leaving a burning red mark in the shape of a handprint along the apple of my cheek. And that same night, before bed, I recall him tearing that same tooth from its root, leaving my pearly whites swimming in a pool of blood like rocks jutting from a raging river of violent red.

Murus was full of lessons like these. By the time I was seven years old, I had learned to manage the pain like a bad cold. It never went away, really, but it did linger, tucked away somewhere in one of the chambers of my heart. Infecting me from the inside out, contaminating the cells of my body, mutating into quieted self-loathing. It was only when my body ached with fatigue, or my instinct to survive kicked in, that the phantom of that pain roared to life, a searing ache that vibrated through my bones.

Yet another one of Murus's renowned mantras: a lesson is only as memorable as its pain. Growing numb to the pain he inflicted on me was my own way of retaliating against him—my refusal to learn from him. There was nothing he could teach me. A woman, biologically weak, inferior to a man like Murus, I had no means of fighting against the force behind his hands. You can't teach somebody to be someone they're not—a *man* that they are not.

Even stronger was the force behind his words, each one wrapped in irritability and tied together with a bow of contempt. Any man—every man—bent to his will, so long as he wished it. They would sooner spit in the face of Death than in the face of his authority.

"To what pleasure do we owe this unexpected visit?" my father asked, drawing out the "pleasure," his smile widening.

A snake with a tongue of literary prowess, empowered by the mind of a dictator.

"I've come to introduce my son." General Salices' voice was edged with hostility contradicted by the glimmer of his warm irises. "As the head of our compound, I thought it only polite to present you with your newest resident."

"Very well." Murus folded his arms across his inflated chest, jutting out his chin. "Is your husband bringing the young lad?"

A fraction of hesitation. The general's lip twitched. "No, no. He's busy running errands, I'm afraid. He extends his apologies."

Murus bowed his head. "A shame."

"I've brought him along myself. Come, Quercus."

General Salices folded his hands together in an effort to compose himself, his tan skin glowing. Pride. A display of affection that I failed to see my own father exhibit. On the rare occasion I did see a hint of his approval, it was because someone had told him something he'd been waiting to hear.

Not that I would do him the favour.

Stepping out of the way, the general revealed the fair-skinned child standing behind him. They had a lick of flame for hair and a hardness to their eyes.

A gulp of breath caught in my throat, blocking my airway. Though it came as no surprise, the Salices' child was a boy.

Compound 43 was occupied by only the most respected citizens of the Ascendancy. Men of the military. Men of science. Political figureheads. Men chock-full of power and superiority, which they'd been entitled to long before they were born and adopted into the force of their domineering lineage.

A ray of the sun's light fell upon the tall boy, casting a golden tone to his broad shoulders. I traced the outline of his set chin and square jaw in my mind, and saplings of panic bloomed in my chest. As much as it pained me to admit it, he was handsome. A quality valued by the Ascendancy. His draw of the genetic roulette wheel demanded respect and trust. As he turned his eyes toward me, taking notice of my prolonged stare, I bowed my head, allowing a curtain of my thick hair to veil my face.

"Why, he's nearly a man," commented Murus dubiously, scratching at this chin.

His doubts were well justified. When a nuptial pair was granted the request to adopt a child, the child they received was typically between the ages of three months and a year old. But the boy standing on our porch—their newest arrival—looked on the brink of his eighteenth year.

The Ascendancy controlled the number of births on an annual basis, according to marital statistics monitored by the administration, to prevent overpopulation. Per these numbers, only a predetermined number of gestational carriers delivered children to be adopted out. It was the natural way of things, a method meant to ensure human prosperity. Overpopulation meant illness to the entire race, as fatal to our survival as the uncontrolled division of cancer cells ravaging the central nervous system. Symptoms included poverty, an upsurge in disease, and malnutrition, amongst others.

Of course, I'd only come to learn this collective knowledge about the Ascendancy within the last two years—beginning with the morning of my eleventh birthday, when I'd awoken to the first signs of pubescence. Murus had wasted no time in warning me about the disgrace that would fall upon our family name should I think to "act promiscuously and fall pregnant with an illegitimate child."

Another one of the Ascendancy's many laws: no heterosexual relations. Natural procreation meant jeopardizing the harmony that the Ascendancy had worked toward over generations, endangering their promise of purity and self-fortification against the forces of genetic mutation.

Fingers prodded my shoulder, urging me forward to greet our new neighbour. I craned my neck to shake my head at Murus, stopping short as he brought his hand up to grip the back of my neck and give it a squeeze. Not hard enough to cause any pain, but with enough force to give my heart a jolt.

My eyes darted from Quercus, to the general, to Murus. "But—" I began to protest until he tightened his fingers, pinching my skin. A warning.

Another impending lesson.

I bit the inside of my cheek, defying the flinch that threatened to yank the muscles in my face. I wouldn't give him the satisfaction of

my submission.

Loosening his grip on my neck, he nudged me forward another step with a stern hand.

"Say hello, Miles," he said, setting his jaw. Something told me that he was on his last nerve.

I wrinkled my nose, trying to mask my embarrassment as I forced myself to stand in front of the Salices boy. "Hello," I blurted.

"Hello."

The general clapped a hand on Quercus' shoulder.

"Don't let him deceive you; he's usually quite a bit of a chatterbox."

I stole a glance at the fiery-haired boy. He stood with a wide stance, his shoulders straight and his pink lips wearing a phantom of a lopsided smile.

"In any case, this is quite the surprise." Murus' eyes tensed as he flashed them a smile, lines carving out the corners of his eyes. "Would you care to join us inside for something to drink?"

The general waved the offer away before lowering himself to my level, resting his forearms on his knees. "Why don't you show my son the sights while your father and I discuss some…business."

Fright seized my lungs and a chill crept along the length of my spine as he pulled his lip back to reveal twisted canines, a snarl disguised as a grin. An order dressed in the cloak of a suggestion.

Nodding my head in compliance, I skittered past the Salices boy and down my front steps, hearing the *click* of the front door shutting behind me as Murus followed the general into our base.

Keenly aware of the footsteps trailing after me, I took in a long breath and closed my eyes, allowing the weight of the earth to guide me as I continued down along the sidewalk. If I pretended that Quercus was a figment of my imagination, only as real as I permitted him to be, I figured that he would be courteous enough to do the same. I'd stay out of his way, and he'd leave my face intact.

When I'd made it ten feet from the foot of our porch, I knelt down to sit on the curb, hugging my knees against my chest.

A front of gray clouds fringed the horizon. As the sun ducked behind the clouds, a dark shadow swallowed the street, now illuminated only by the morsel of light that peeked through the overcast skies.

The sound of someone clearing their throat made me jump. Without looking over my shoulder, I could tell that Quercus was standing over me, just by the outline of his body shadowing the corners of my vision. But I kept silent. As far as I was concerned, he was just another potential bully. And I worried that if I paid him any sort of kindliness, he'd work to make it known that men and women weren't meant to be friends. It was easier for everyone if I knew my place.

Beneath them.

Without invitation, Quercus moved to sit on the curb beside me, leaning back and laying his palms flat against the sidewalk. I swallowed, keeping my eye on him.

Why did he have to sit so close, anyhow? There was an entire stretch of curb he could have sat on, but for whatever reason he'd seated himself next to me, inches away—a mode of intimidation or assertion, perhaps. Serving as a reminder that men owned the very ground I invaded upon.

I began to get up, using one hand to push myself up from the ground. Before I'd made it to my feet, a firm hand gripped my wrist, sending my heart into a jackhammering frenzy. Quercus gazed calmly at me, and I dreaded the way my nerves roared to life.

"Are you afraid of me?"

The question struck me like a thorn, pricking my skin all over. My palms were tacky, my lower lip quivering. I tried to gather saliva in my mouth, as though I'd ingested a mouthful of sand. My tongue was a dead weight in my mouth as I tried to formulate a response.

"Shouldn't I be?"

ONE

MILES

Ten years later

"Health care was, indeed, the world's greatest plague," emphasized the broadcaster. The words, both religiously over-rehearsed and hysterically ironic, were the word of law. They were essential to that segment of the broadcast, which was regularly looped on the date of the *Regeneratio*. It ensured that we, as registered citizens, acknowledged our distinguished history.

The man's monotone voice rang in my ears as I scratched the tip of my pencil to my paper, logging my day's events with careful precision. With my nose mere inches from the desktop I worked at, the edge of my hand smudging the granite alloy, it wasn't until an almost inaudible mutter caught my attention that my head snapped up in the direction of Murus's office.

His voice boomed as one of the doors flung open, his cheeks blotchy with the blood rising to the surface of his face.

"I don't give a rat's a—"

He had begun to raise his voice when he caught sight of me, after which he cut himself short. He ran his calloused hands over his well-kept button-down shirt and adjusted his tie at the knot, then gave a husky-looking man—who I inferred to be one of his many business associates—a curt nod.

The associate was tall and wearing a grey suit. His hair was ebony black, and there was a red mark on his chin from where he'd nicked himself during that morning's shave. Though he was probably years younger than Murus, his bold, bushy eyebrows, drawn together, made him appear much older.

Judging by the hostility that clung to the air surrounding them, I was sure that their quarrel had only just begun. Nevertheless, the unfamiliar man was quick to turn away and see himself out.

I pondered the idea of asking Murus about his day for a flicker in time, but quickly waved away the thought. Politics were not an interest of mine, nor was his schedule.

"You're home rather early." He adjusted the cuffs of his dress shirt, raising his chin to admire himself in the mirror mounted in the hall.

"It's nine p.m.," I informed him, shooting a look at the clock ticking away on the dining room wall. It had been nearly four hours since I had returned home from my leisure—free time designated by the Ascendancy. I'd spent most of it hidden away under the shade of a tree, drawing doodles on the back cover of my logbook.

He bowed his head. "I must have lost track of time."

The pencil clicked gently against the desk's surface as I laid it flat, my palm holding it in place to keep it from rolling over the edge.

It was as though the older man was trapped in a daze as he approached me from behind, his eyelids fluttering with considerable thought.

"What do you have there?"

I tried not to flinch as he rested a hand on my shoulder, running his thumb back and forth. The gesture was normally considered an act of comfort. But for me, it was an act of warning. A reminder that I was under his thumb and his authority. My body, my material being, belonged to him.

My eyes fell to my scrawled-on paper. It was creased where my hand had slipped whenever I'd erased a misspelling or word that, despite being spelt correctly, didn't look quite right.

"Just today's logs," I replied, turning my body so that my arm shielded my heavily guarded thoughts. My body might have been his, but my thoughts were my own. At least for now.

He nodded, scratching at his five o'clock shadow. Murus, as the vice-chancellor of state, was a man of professional standing. In fact, he was what historians would have referred to as "a man of royal stature"; a respectable figure to the public eye. It was rare that he failed to keep his appearance up to standard.

The notion that something was weighing heavily enough on his mind that he had begun to neglect his usual routine brought a frown to my lips. Though we had become almost strangers since my late dad's passing, Murus' outbursts growing more violent and more frequent, there was still a thorn of myself—a little girl trapped inside the body of a woman—that cared for him. Murus was the only piece of my dad that I had left, just as I was the only person on this planet that signified his having existed at all.

After my late dad had been euthanized, Murus chose to put that piece of his life behind him. And by regulation of the Ascendancy, speaking of those euthanized was forbidden. Their identities are destroyed. Families aren't so much as allowed to hold a memorial, or mourn. Life resumes as though the dead never existed at all.

"I spoke to the Salices earlier today," I started, tearing the most recent page out of my logbook. Folding the paper into as tiny a square as I could manage, I tucked the page into the back pocket of my pants. Rising from my spot at the table, I quickly pulled my locks into a ponytail at the nape of my neck. Flyaway hairs had been tickling my face, but I had been too engulfed in my writing to smooth

them back.

"All is well, I hope?" Seating himself across from me, Murus folded his hands together and raised an eyebrow.

"They believe Quercus to be ill," I answered.

I wrapped my arms around myself, unable to tear my gaze away from my feet. I allowed my head to droop on my shoulders, fearing that my legs would grow numb and topple me at the thought of the young man's depleting health.

Murus leaned forward. His face was painted with a tight-lipped smile. "How so?"

"He's run a fever," I explained. "Fell unconscious halfway through this morning's patrol." Squeezing my eyes shut, I fought against the image of his pale face as it formed in my mind.

"And?"

"That's all I know."

Murus rose to his feet, moving to stand in front of me.

"Oh, dear. That's quite unfortunate, wouldn't you say?" He rested his hands on my shoulders, lowering his head to look me in the eye. I bit the inside of my cheek as I tried not to shrug out from under his grasp. "That Salices kid was a hardworking young man."

Was.

I flinched at his inclination to speak of the man's life in the past tense, as though Quercus had already faced diagnosis.

A citizen's diagnosis was synonymous with a crime punishable by nothing less than death. When a citizen exhibited symptoms of illness, it was required by law that they report to their designated laboratory to be tested for various diseases catalogued within the database's archives, which dated back hundreds of years. Their prognosis would either be denied or confirmed, the latter of the two meaning immediate euthanasia. It was a system put in place by the Ascendancy as a means of protecting us from the risk of disease. An act of purification and human resilience. A sick human was a weak

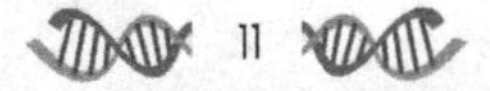

human—a threat to the security of our species.

This information had been ingrained in my mind from the time I was old enough to comprehend general knowledge. It was what was best for the Ascendancy. Healthy citizens with little chance of catching illness meant a robust, efficient, and progressive economy. Citizens with impeccable health could configure their knowledge in their specific fields and work proactively under their assigned roles. It meant survival of the fittest, as marked in every history textbook known to our genetically enhanced humanity.

As for my role? I'd yet to figure that out. I wasn't so certain that I was even fit enough to survive, never mind serve as a functioning cog in the Ascendancy's machine.

Knowing that my childhood friend—who I hadn't seen in nearly a decade—was potentially hours from his time of death, my skin crawled. The systems in place were meant to ensure safety. But at that moment, I didn't feel safe. My stomach only distorted with nausea as the faint memory of my distant childhood, my first meeting with Quercus, boiled to the surface.

Are you afraid of me? his voice echoed in my skull.

I didn't know what came over me, but I knew that I couldn't stop myself.

"You have to do something," I pleaded with the voice of a defenseless little girl. Not a twenty-two-year-old woman or the daughter of one of the most powerful men on the planet, but a young, fatherless girl about to lose the only friend she'd ever known.

My fingers curled into the fabric of my white shirt. I couldn't see my own face, but I knew that my complexion was whitening as the heat drained from my skin. The contents of my stomach curdled.

When I was a young girl, Murus had reassured me that he would stop at nothing to benefit my happiness. A father's word. But the current lack of compassion in his black eyes left a painful lump in my throat.

"It's out of my hands," he said, igniting my bones so that they scorched me from the inside out. Nothing was out of his hands. Not since Dad's passing and Murus' subsequent promotion.

How could he lie to my face? Though the question dangled from my mind, I already knew the answer. Murus didn't care about the truth unless it benefited him or the prosperity of the Ascendancy. There hadn't been trust between us since…

I ground my teeth, trying to keep my rage from tainting my tone of voice. I grabbed him by the elbow as he began to pull away, ready to return to his office.

"You owe him my life."

Without a moment's hesitation, Murus had backed me up against our dining room table. His hand trembled as he lifted it to my face, and I could have sworn he was going to strike me. My heart, as well as my small frame, sank into a pathetic pool on the floor. Arms shielding my head, I broke out into a cry, unable to contain the shuddering of my body as I sobbed into the hardwood.

"I owe nobody. Not Quercus, and *especially* not you!" shouted Murus, spraying beads of saliva into my face as he seized my arms and jerked me toward him.

Hot breath beat against my face, and panic swelled in my chest. There was a wildness in his eyes that seared into my own. In their dark, murky depths was a reflection. My eyes, rounder than I'd ever seen them before, stared back at me. They were the eyes of prey caught in a dense thicket, a creature whose ankle had gotten tangled up in an exposed tree root. I was thrashing, a scream growing in my lungs. There was no escape. And if I didn't kick myself loose, he was going to kill me.

It wouldn't be the first time he'd threaten to revoke my privilege to live.

I waited for the impact of his fists beating against my jaw and for the blooms of bruises to mark my pale skin in places no one would ever see or look. But before either of us could peep another word or move another muscle, an alert blared on the display across the room.

Murus let his hands drop from my arms and clenched his fists as he gazed at the screen. I wasn't sure whether it was the way the light faded from his eyes or the way his lower lip quivered, but I knew something was wrong.

Encouraged by his sudden vulnerability, I propped myself up on my knees to peer at the screen myself. My heartbeat ceased, and the surrounding air nipped at my skin like frost.

TWO

SILENS

ROUTINE. THEY SAY IT'S GOOD FOR THE SOUL. Brings certitude and relief to those who can't stop moving, thinking, *doing*, even for a moment.

He was not one of those people.

Every morning was the same laid-out, bland cycle of events.

Wake up, get dressed, patrol. Return to base, steal a quick nap, patrol some more. Then join his parents for supper later in the evening and get into a heated argument about an expectation that he failed to live up to.

Patrol. Patrol. Patrol.

And by then the day was over, devoid of any real meaning. As an Arxman, his sworn duty was to protect his peers and the civilians that occupied their tunnels. This duty was how Arxmen repaid their leader, the Director, for founding the Resiliens. For offering a safe haven to the inhuman and those in alliance with them. And though Treyton wasn't inhuman, he was an ally. Nobody deserved to have their lives taken from them for being something they did not ask to be.

But that particular morning, clambering out of bed and pulling his shirt over his head, something seemed different. Maybe it was something in the air, or maybe he had pulled a neck muscle in his sleep. Maybe the little man wandering around in his brain was tripping wires, removing them and placing them elsewhere. But something *was* different. Something about today was unusual. It was an unexplainable feeling that weighed on his mind, whispering the possibility of transformation in his ear.

Retrieving his footgear from where he had kicked them off before curling up in bed after a long, tedious patrol, he pulled them on, yanking the straps tight. The resistant, molecularly-altered anthene textile hugged the muscles extending midway over his thighs.

Almost all gear manufactured and provided by the Resiliens, the governing council of their opposing version of the widespread Ascendancy, had been designed to cover and protect every inch of an Arxman's skin while still providing him with the luxury of an unlimited range of motion. Anthene was native to the earth beneath the tunnels—their home. Naturally, the material was lightweight and flexible. Molecular scientists much more brilliant than himself had altered the material so that it was resistant to trauma. If they had one advantage over the Ascendancy, it was the material that made up their uniforms, the very shell on their backs. Though it was thin enough to be pierced with enough force in close-range combat, it was a layer of difference between life and death.

As he twisted his body to peer at his bed, the covers still folded back and his pillows askew, the material of his second skin morphed to his shape. He rolled his shoulders back before stretching his arms over his head, letting out a gaping yawn.

A yellow, blinking light out of the corner of his eye made him snap his head in the direction of his bedside table. His phone, waiting patiently for him, was the source of the blinking, indicating new correspondence. But before he had made it a step toward the device, a harsh knock jarred his bedroom door.

"Open up!"

The voice on the other side of the door could only belong to one person. A balmy flicker of revulsion burrowed deeper into Treyton's gut as he twisted the doorknob and waited.

There was a *thud* against the steel as his brother tried to fling it open from the outside with the brute strength of his body. Little did he know that days before, after James had awoken him in that same manner, Treyton had reversed the hinges on his door so that the door would swing out rather than in. With an amused snort, he used the toe of his foot to kick the door forward and send his pest of an older sibling stumbling further out into the narrow tunnel.

Buckled over in a fit of laughter, he didn't realize that James was standing over him until he cleared his throat. When Treyton regarded him, unable to wipe the smirk from the lower half of his face, James folded his arms over his broad chest, his brows drawn together.

He was a big guy despite standing half a foot shorter than Treyton did. At six years Treyton's senior, he'd had more years of training, workouts, and patrolling. He knew the ins and outs of the tunnels even better than Treyton did. All of that was what made Treyton's victory, though small, all the more satisfying.

Their fathers respected James. He was their pride and joy; their not-so-baby boy. Rule-abiding, arrogant, stern. There were only so many words Treyton could use to describe his brother. But above all else, he was dedicated. Loyal. In fact, he was so dedicated to the origins of his life that he refused to respond to anything other than his birth-given Ascendant name: Currens. If anyone was going to follow in their parents' footsteps should something drastic—God forbid—happen to them, it would be him.

Not Treyton.

Not that he wanted to follow in their footsteps. He was his own person; a rogue at heart. They needed him more than he needed them. He played no part in their social hierarchy. He was a lone wolf patrolling the borders with a thirst for the thrill of the fight. Whether he won or lost was besides the point.

"*Irrumabo,* Silens, did you reverse the hinges on your door?"

Did James want him to spell it out for him? Or was he playing dumb in an attempt to make him feel guilty?

Treyton grit his teeth, holding his brother's stare. The depths of Treyton's eyes were hot with expressive blue flame. He didn't answer the question. He wouldn't give him the satisfaction of an answer.

Tensing his jaw, James elbowed past him, inviting himself into his room. His stern eyes scanned the bed, the desk pressed up against the adjacent wall, and the floor, almost as though he was expecting to find something of concern.

"And why haven't you been answering your communications device?"

Treyton, again, didn't answer. He didn't owe him an explanation as to where he had been and why he did or didn't answer his phone. Despite what James seemed to believe, he wasn't his commanding officer. He was just a man who had escaped the face of danger alongside their parents. In simpler terms, he'd gotten lucky. And apparently that warranted being an invasive pain in Treyton's ass.

"Silens," James called. The name grated against Treyton's nerves. He had been called many names, all of which he preferred over *that* one.

"Don't call me that, for Christ's sake," he said, moving to fall back onto his mattress with a theatrical sigh.

Silens. His pseudonym among those in the Ascendancy. Due to their family's history, it was a name he knew too well and heard too frequently. Before the Ascendancy's *Regeneratio,* the Venus couple—his fathers—and their four-year-old, James, had held no loyalty toward the Resiliens. They'd been ordinary citizens registered under the Ascendancy, living an everyday life in the fourteenth compound.

Well, as normal as an everyday life could be under the laws and leadership of the Ascendancy. They'd been fortunate enough that they weren't penniless like those within the compounds classified by a lower, singular digit, and made do with the company they found in one another.

It was not until the laws that they had centered their entire existence around began to waver, endangering James' life, that they had sought refuge elsewhere.

His condition, if discovered, would have been immediate cause for euthanasia under order of the Ascendancy; yet fleeing their previous home, a memory that Treyton had attained only through storytelling, had nursed little influence on James' character. After all these years—twenty-two, to be exact—and despite his time in their current civilization, James seemed still to be a citizen of the Ascendancy at heart. If it were not for the safety that the Resiliens ensured, Treyton thought that James could have walked a very different path. One that would have altered the fate of their current home.

The haunting history that loomed over Treyton's family's reputation had wedged an expanding rift between him and his brother as the years had progressed. While Treyton found mentorship in his Resiliens counterparts, embracing their modern take on life, James never followed suit. He was withdrawn, isolating himself from others. And in situations where cooperation was expected—necessary, even—he complied begrudgingly, as though the entire world had somehow cheated him and beaten him into a solitary life.

Day-to-day life for James consisted of a series of missions yet to be accomplished. And he wouldn't rest until those tasks were completed. Today's task: the long-awaited initiation of the *Res Novae*, meaning "the political revolution."

The reminder dawned on Treyton, shedding a light of

understanding over his mind. That was why today had seemed different.

Today marked the beginning of the war the Resiliens had been preparing to fight for over two decades.

The sole goal of the Resiliens, whose name translated loosely to "the rebellion of the resilient," was to weaken the Ascendancy's defences and eliminate the false reality that they'd created regarding the history of humanity. And the only reasonable way to do this was to debilitate their citizens' belief systems so that their trust would waver, leaving way for the truth to enlighten them and alleviate their confusion. Today, their fathers' plan would set it in motion.

Sitting up to kneel on his bed, both hands resting on his thighs to keep himself balanced, Treyton eyed his brother.

"What brings you to my humble quarters?" he asked.

"'Humble' isn't the word I would use." James gestured to the collection of self-portraits that Treyton had on display in a glass cabinet next to his dresser. "Vain is more like it. Certainly not humble."

Treyton folded his arms. "I think someone's upset that he didn't make it into my cabinet of favourite things." A smug grin tugged at the corners of his mouth.

"Your"—James paused, as though searching for the right word—"*portfolio* is the least of my worries."

Retrieving Treyton's phone from off his nightstand, James turned it over a few times in his hands. "Your communications device appears to be in working order. So why haven't you been responding to my correspondence?"

"I've been busy."

"With?"

"Making tiny paper cranes."

"Origami?"

"God bless you."

Treyton threw his legs over the edge of his bed, rubbing his eyes with the back of his hands to clear the remaining fuzziness of sleep from his eyes. "Look, man. If you're that lonely, we could always get you a puppy. A nice fluffy one. You could sniff each other's as—"

Without a word of warning, James propelled the phone in his direction, startling him into action. Treyton sprung up, catching his phone and cradling it to his chest before tucking it into one of his many pants pockets, safe against another one of James's outbursts.

"As much as I appreciate the sentiment and all, save the game of catch for you and your furry friend. And for future reference," he said, "my phone is not a ball." Though he was careful to keep his tone comical, ballooning frustration laced his words.

Circling the room, his eyes still searching, James stopped in the doorway before staring pointedly at him. "Are you done?"

Treyton basked in gratification. James' ordinarily perfect composure was cracking under the pressure of his brazenness.

He hopped off his bed, retrieving his jacket from where it was slung over the headboard and slipping it on. He tugged the material to loosen any bunching, then ran his hands over the front of the jacket. The embellishments felt like pebbles under his palms.

"For now," Treyton answered, shooting James his widest grin. "I was sleeping."

James furrowed his brow. "Pardon me?"

"You asked why I wasn't answering my texts," he reminded him, clipping him in the shoulder as he pushed his way through the doorway next to him. "I only woke up a few minutes before you came and assaulted my poor, oblivious door."

Treyton raised his arms above his head, pretending to cower from James to replicate how his door might have responded to James's tantrum had it sprouted limbs as well as a consciousness.

James glowered at him, unimpressed with his reenactment.

"Please, sir," Treyton cried out, raising the pitch of his voice to feign vulnerable innocence. "Don't hurt me! I'm just an innocent door minding his own hinges!"

Treyton moved to block his exposed torso, but James was faster. Before Treyton could flinch, James drove his fist into his gut. The air forced out of his lungs, Treyton cradled his abdomen as he buckled into the fetal position on the floor. His lungs ached against every breath, and his diaphragm was hard as a sack of rocks as it struggled against relaxation.

After a long moment, he was able to breathe steadily again. Locking eyes with James, he said, "You break it, you buy it."

Ignoring Treyton's remark, James wrapped a hand around his forearm and hauled him to his feet.

"Pater and Tata are holding a meeting regarding the first stages of the Res Novae. We're already late, so quit dawdling."

THREE

SILENS

THE TUNNELS HAD BEEN HIS HOME since the moment he was born. He had been brought to life within these tunnels, and he vowed to die within them if he could manage it. That was, as long as an Ascendant officer didn't get to him first.

The trip to the conference room where their fathers anticipated their arrival was a fifteen-minute walk from Treyton's room, which was located in one of the many residential sectors. The complex system of tunnels made up the underground base that they, the civilians of the Resiliens, had called home for generations; a safe haven reinforced by steel and concrete. The air in the tunnels was cool and crisp. Nothing like you might expect from air dozens of feet below the surface of the earth. It was refreshing against his bare forearms.

Blue light, installed years before either he or James were born, poured out over the tunnels, illuminating the cement walls towering around them. Bright enough to illuminate the dark depths of their underground world, yet dim enough that it deluded their eyes, making the world seem almost cataclysmic. And in a way, it was.

Civilians remembered very little about life above ground. And those that did, like Treyton, who patrolled above ground on a regular basis, only knew fear.

Anticipation.

The need to survive.

When they arrived at the conference room, he and James made their way inside, careful not to make any noise so as not to interrupt the happenings inside and draw attention to their tardiness.

A camera suspended from the ceiling above them whirred to life and swivelled in their immediate direction. Treyton bit back a curse word under the knowledge that he was being recorded against his will.

Next to him, James paid the camera no mind. Either because he wasn't aware of its existence or because he didn't care whether or not his every move was recorded. Nor should he. Nobody suspected that he would act out. He was their golden boy, after all.

James continued onward, maintaining the balance in his broad shoulders. He seated himself opposite their parents at the conference table amongst the other Arxmen, each of whom was the head of their own respective department. Alessandra, Orio, and Eyre, to list a few Treyton recognized, were present. They were all familiar faces, mentors that he had grown up alongside, respected, and admired.

Even loved.

Treyton's eyes wandered to study Klara's face as she lifted her head, her round eyes catching his. He knew Klara best of them all.

Before he could finish reading her expression, the tightness in her gaze alluding to something out of the ordinary, she turned her cheek to him.

Odd.

The door was still cracked open behind him, invading the room with a blue sliver of light that sliced the room in half.

Now that everybody had recognized Treyton's added presence,

there was no sense in trying to be quiet. Grabbing the door handle behind him and yanking the door shut, he leaned into the steel. He welcomed the cool sensation against his back, which was sweating against their scrutiny. Tension coiled itself around his throat like a snake, threatening to constrict if he didn't choose his words wisely.

The tectonics under his feet shifted, and his words split the silence of the room. "Good morning."

A sensation like claws raking his spine sent a shiver through him.

Tata lifted himself from his seat with a grunt of effort to look him in the eye. He hesitated a moment before bowing his head in greeting. As usual, his beard was trimmed, and he was dressed in a tailored suit. Every button was done up except for the top, hinting at the white dress shirt he wore underneath. As the head of their family name, the man was always dressed to impress. The responsibility of executive decisions on behalf of the Resiliens rested upon his experienced shoulders.

Treyton hoped he'd never have to shoulder the burden of that job.

Cold air washed over him, and another wave of shivers gripped him, causing the hair along his arms to prickle, alert. Shaking his head, Treyton tried to focus on the table of people, now expressing their concern with offered frowns. But his thoughts were drowned out, overwhelmed by the *thud-thud-thudding* of his heart. Blood roared in his ears.

Tata's face was still and unchanging. Another chill made Treyton squirm in his boots, the tips of his fingers numb from the cold. The frost smothered every inch of his body, the tips of his ears aching. He couldn't see them, but he knew they were red.

Had no one else noticed the drop in temperature? Rubbing his arms for warmth, he searched the room for an explanation: an open air vent or a fan. But there was no apparent reason for the change in temperature, and nobody else seemed to be bothered.

With a frown, Pater took his husband's hand in his own, urging him back into his seat. Then he nodded his head at the open seat next to him. "Why don't you take a seat, son?"

Treyton moved to stand closer to his family at their corner of the table so that he could engage in the inevitable conversation without straying too far from the door, but he scrutinized the offered seat with a wary mind.

A soft ringing sounded. The heads in the room turned toward the sound and an apologetic Klara, who had sunk back into her chair. "Sorry," she said before putting the phone to her ear, whispering into the microphone. After a few inaudible words were exchanged, she gripped the phone tightly in her hand and rose from her chair.

"I apologize for the interruption, but I have a patient calling for me back at the infirmary."

A look of understanding crossed over Treyton's fathers' faces, though he could see Tata wrinkle his lip a little. Klara excused herself from the room, shutting the door behind her. There was a twinge in Treyton's chest, followed by the urge to string along after her. But he knew that if he did, he would be making a poor example of himself. One that would confirm the others' doubts about him.

It was not until Tata had settled back into his seat, finding comfort in Pater's presence, that James decided to speak up. "It is with our sincerity that we apologize for our tardiness," he said, addressing the room.

James leaned back in his chair, making himself comfortable despite the distress coming off their parents in waves powerful enough to knock Treyton off his feet. Teeth chattering in his mouth, Treyton's offense at him speaking on his behalf was submerged by the quick, short sounds of enamel on enamel.

"That's quite all right, James," Pater said.

The Arxmen at the table engaged in small talk, greeting one another and discussing the latest developments within their departments. But the words melted together into nothing but incoherent babbling. All Treyton could focus on was the shooting pain in his arms as the cold air beat against his skin.

As the babbling increased, the temperature continued to plummet.

"Enough!" Treyton snapped finally and threw up his hands, unable to manage the shooting pain in his fingers and toes. If no one else was going to address the elephant in the room, he guessed he was going to have to take on the responsibility. After all, his reputation for stirring conflict amongst the rest of them preceded him.

"Is this supposed to be some kind of trick?" Treyton forced a loud, strained laugh, feigning amusement. "Because it's hilarious!"

All eyes turned to stare in his direction, bewildered. James stood up to reach for his arm in a disciplinary manner, his brow furrowed and his lips pressed tightly together, but Treyton was quick to swat away his outstretched hand.

"What are you talking about?" Alessandra's face hardened as she got up to circle about the room.

"You can't feel it?" The pitch of his voice escaped him, growing higher as panic began to rattle his nerves. A list of reasonable explanations—illness, anemia—whirled about in his mind. But a gut instinct told him that what he was experiencing wasn't the typical seasonal flu. Were they ignoring it, or were they oblivious to it?

No, there was no way they didn't feel it. His fingers should have been turning blue with hypothermia, yet their olive colouring remained.

Looking startled, an expression that he seldom wore, James let his hand fall still at his side. Pater, meanwhile, pushed himself out of his chair and made his way around the side of the table to stand in front of Treyton. Hastily pressing one wrist to his forehead, Pater brought his other hand up to the side of Treyton's throat. His lip movements echoed his thoughts as he checked his pulse, concentration forming

lines on his forehead.

"You're unusually warm. Any signs of dizziness or blocked sinuses?"

With a shake of his head, Treyton withdrew from his father's touch.

"I felt fine until I walked in," he answered honestly. And while the spiral of panic he had been descending into was still a phantom lingering behind his ribcage, it had melted into something softer. Warmer, even.

Stretching out his arms, Treyton was surprised to find that the little hairs lay flat again.

Trying to hide the confusion in his voice as he spoke next, Treyton shifted closer to the exit. "The sooner you tell us why we're all here, the sooner I can go back to my room."

Tata slammed his fist against the table, startling the others. He ran his fingers through his graying hair, avoiding the looks of his peers and family members.

"This isn't a good idea," he said, raising his voice. "Sending him out into the field while he's in this state could cost us everything we've worked for!"

"I know you're frustrated, my love," Pater soothed, taking his husband's hands in his own from the opposite side of the table. "But at least let me explain to them. We can have Trey pay a visit to the infirmary afterward and, if he is truly ill, we'll find a substitute to fill his absence."

A substitute. Treyton snorted.

Tata leaned back in his chair, allowing his fingers to slip away from Pater's. Treyton took a breath, hoping he could control his temper long enough to escape the obligation of the meeting.

Taking a stand at the head of the table with a small device, a remote, in hand, Pater pulled up a screen full of information behind him. In the upper right-hand corner of the screen was an image of a girl with long, wiry hair and milky skin. Something about her features seemed familiar, the darkness in her eyes unsettling.

Treyton skimmed the lines of information. She was two years older than him, which was surprisingly young. Only twenty-two years old. Not the age of their usual quarry.

"Who is she?" James asked, watching the screen.

An intense wave of curiosity emitted from his brother, striking Treyton in the chest. Stumbling, he stretched an arm to catch himself against the wall before the others took notice.

Come on, body. What's up with you?

"As you all know, Murus Amissa is the vice-chancellor within the Ascendancy," Tata said. "*This* is Miles Amissa, his only adopted child. A daughter. You will be kidnapping her, with her consent, and bringing her back to base."

Treyton winced, clenching his teeth against the rush of heat to his body. The undeniable urge to beat something to a pulp gripped him.

"You can't be serious." James raised his voice, startling the gathered department heads seated on either side of him. "You want us to kidnap a high-class citizen, never mind an innocent girl? Why her and not somebody more…important?"

Between gasps, fighting off a rapid wave of lightheadedness, Treyton seized the opportunity to poke fun at his brother. Anything to lighten the air.

"A girl? Take another look at her, bro. She's all woman." Had Klara still been present, she might have scoffed.

James clenched his fist, working diligently to ignore his remark. He reverted his attention back to their parents. "You plan to send us into the heart of enemy grounds, somehow hoping we make it out of there alive with a captive?"

Pater removed the glasses inching down the bridge of his nose and folded them in his hands. The dark frames were worn from years of use, the lenses marked with fingerprints. Nearsightedness, developed in his young adulthood, was one of many undesirable genetic traits that the Ascendancy frowned upon. Had it not been for his wit, or for his courage, Pater would have been euthanized long before he'd even gotten married.

"You two are our world," Pater said. "Our reason for fighting on behalf of the Resiliens. I don't *want* to send you two into dangerous territory, Currens. But you're the only Arxmen we can trust with this task."

"So why the girl? Why not Murus himself?" Treyton cut in, steadying himself. Whatever had knocked the wind out of him had ceased.

"The Ascendancy does not value their women to the same degree that they value their men. Miles is the only female of high status. Her capture will be enough to stir the pot, so to speak, while also buying us enough time for the next phase of our plan."

James propped himself against the table, his chin resting in his hand. "You mentioned that she would have to come willingly. Kind of defeats the idea of a kidnapping, don't you think? How can we even be certain that she will comply?"

With the press of a button, the screen behind Pater flipped to a new set of information. Treyton skimmed through the heap of text, his eyes narrowing as they stumbled upon another image. A young man with fiery red hair and sunken-in cheeks was crouched alongside a wire fence, hardly holding himself upright. Blood trailed from a laceration on his forehead, just above his left eye, and the exposed parts of his body were painted with yellow and purple blotches. Bruises. Surrounding him were a patrol of Ascendant military officers.

"Quercus Salices, one of our former informants. At the age of twelve—the beginning of his training—we lost communications with him and his patrol not long after they were dispatched. But recently, he's resurfaced in our systems."

Tata had gotten up from his chair and was now pacing up and down the length of the conference table as he spoke. Concern had twisted his expression into something beyond recognition. Treyton watched him, aware of the somersaults his stomach was doing. The sensation grew so overwhelming that he quivered in his boots.

"Given the buildup you've provided, I'm going to assume that you've gotten word on the status of their relationship?" James said.

Pater perked up, seeming impressed by James's observational skills. "Precisely, Currens. Due to an incident in their youth, it appears that Miss Amissa holds some loyalty toward Mister Salices."

"And Mister Salices is facing a death sentence as we speak," Tata chimed in, his grin unnerving. "We've taken care of all the technicalities. All you need to do is go and retrieve her from her base. The coordinates have been sent to your devices."

Treyton thanked their ancestors in silence. What probably had been fifteen minutes had seemed like a full turn of the clock, but the meeting was finally drawing to a close.

Once Treyton had made a quick visit to Klara in her infirmary and received medical clearance—standard protocol before going out into the field, if illness was suspected—he and James could be on their way and he would be free from the unusual aura in the room. Just as he turned to excuse himself, however, James raised another question.

Of course.

"Why did no one ever try to recover the boy? You've been keeping tabs on him, but for what? General curiosity?" His brother tapped a finger to his chin, eyeing the screen with a raised brow. Treyton could tell by his scowl that he had his suspicions.

Tata forced a chuckle. "Of all people, you should understand that risking countless lives for the sake of one is outright foolish. If we could survey him from afar, his death at least might not be in vain. Which has proven true, seeing as his prior relationship to the girl will help us further our plan along."

Gratification rang in Treyton's ears. The blood coursing through his body brought a rush of warmth to the tips of his ears. A flush crawled across the high points of his cheeks. The fervent presence of emotion was cause enough for his heart to beat hard against the inside of his chest.

Cursing under his breath, Treyton scratched the top of his head, using his raised arm to shield as much of his face as possible.

What the hell is happening to me?

Leaving a kiss on his beloved's cheek, Pater excused himself from the room to attend to other assumed responsibilities.

"Alessandra will give you a rundown of your assignment before you leave base," Tata said. With that, he followed after his husband, but not without first ruffling the hair on James' head.

The other department heads began to file out the door. On her way out, Alessandra leaned to whisper something in James' ear, to which he responded with a curt nod.

When the brothers were the only two remaining people in the room, James moved to join Treyton by the door.

"Are you sure you are fit to report to your duties?" he queried, lowering his voice to a whisper should any remaining Arxmen linger outside.

"Fit as a dog."

Treyton forced a smile to not only provoke his brother, but to distract himself from his own thoughts. Whatever it was that was manipulating him had to be temporary, seeing as it had only taken effect a few moments after they'd entered the room.

A freak of nature, like déjà vu.

FOUR

SILENS

NUDGING OPEN THE INFIRMARY DOOR, Treyton held the air in his lungs captive as he peered inside. Standing on the opposite end of the room was Klara. She was bent over a young girl, pressing a hand against the girl's small, bandaged wrist.

"Try to be more careful next time, all right, hon?" Reaching forward, Klara brushed the girl's auburn hair out of her red, puffy eyes.

Nodding, the young girl gathered her small quilted blanket in her arms. Treyton refrained from scrunching up his face as she wiped her leaky nose on the back of her hand. Then, without so much as a peep, she vanished through another exit out of his line of view.

Once he was sure that Klara was no longer tending to any other patients, he made his arrival known with a forced cough.

"What can I do for you today?" she asked, her back turned to him as she shuffled through a stack of files. As usual, her mind was so centered on the work in front of her that she didn't realize it was he who had entered the room.

Walking up behind her, his chest brushing up against her

shoulders, Treyton wrapped his arms around her and covered her eyes with both hands. Lowering his mouth to her ear, he whispered, "Guess who?"

Files slipped out of her hands, and papers glided to the floor around their feet. Whirling on him, a coy smile tugged at her lips.

"You could have just said something, Ton."

Treyton knelt to help her retrieve the scattered documents, sorting them into their appropriate folders. "Sorry about this," he said, gesturing to the floor where a few loose spreadsheets remained.

"You'd better be. Let me see where I put my paper clips." She hurried into another room in the back, her white medical coat sweeping the floor behind her like a cape.

As Treyton set the last folder on her desk, a familiar name written on the front in black marker caught his attention.

AMISSA—URGENT

"What is this?" he called out to her, opening it to look at the first document that stared up at him: a birth certificate processed and signed by a governing member of the Ascendancy.

"Your parents asked me to put together any information I could find on a list of citizens they sent me this morning," she called back, poking her head out from behind the door that read *MEDICAL PERSONNEL ONLY.* "They didn't explain why, just that they needed it as soon as I could get my hands on it. Something about your assignment, I think."

Flipping to the next page, a shock rippled through him. It was a document proclaiming a tier-five ability, followed by a detailed description that seemed to include a brief explanation of strengths, weaknesses, effectiveness, and more.

This Amissa daughter was an inhuman, then— a person born by natural circumstances who carried the inhumanus gene. The abilities varied, but usually developed by the age of maturity.

Klara was an inhuman. She possessed the skill to know and

understand something by merely reading, hearing, or touching material found in the archives. Subjects such as human biology or medicine came naturally to her, allowing her to practise medical procedures and perform as the Resiliens' chief physician.

Every inhuman inborn talent was ranked within five tiers, with tier one being an ability with the least capability and five being the most powerful.

Klara's skill fell into the third tier, meaning that her capabilities were beyond that of someone with the capability of flight—a tier-one skill.

A tier-five ability had only ever been a theoretical possibility.

Until now.

Before Treyton could analyze the information on the document and commit it to memory, Klara plucked it from his grasp and whisked the file under her arm.

"You're here for a reason, so spit it out."

Yanking on his ear, she lowered his head to her eye level and began performing a routine evaluation. Eyes, ears, the works.

"I felt off during my briefing with the fam," he explained as she took his pulse, pretending not to notice when she wrinkled her nose in reaction to his use of the word "fam."

"I'm fine now, but they need you to clear me before I can go out into the field with Currens. Standard boring protocol. No biggie."

Her eyes snapped up to look at him. "You and Currens? In the field? Together?"

"Did I stutter?" A corner of his mouth perked.

Shaking her head, she pulled a thermometer from her pocket and motioned for him to open his mouth before placing it under his tongue. He recoiled at the metallic taste.

"They didn't tell you?"

"I've been a little preoccupied," Klara admitted. "It's just..." A pause. "You two aren't exactly a match made in heaven. Currens must be thrilled."

"I made sure to get under his skin a little," Treyton admitted around his mouthful of metal, not ashamed of his natural-born ability to pester his brother with ease. "But our parents trust us, y'know?"

Klara stepped back to hold herself upright against her desk. "So, you're going, then?"

"Well, duh."

His muscles tensed when he noticed her grave expression. It was out of character for her to be so worried about his well-being this way. He had gone out into the field hundreds of times before, and never once had she seemed this uncertain about the matter.

"Am I clear to go?" he asked cautiously.

A beep signalled that the thermometer had finished its reading. She plucked it from his mouth to show him the result: a healthy temperature. Tossing the used thermometer into a biohazardous waste bin at the foot of the bed nearest to them, she buried her hands in her coat pockets.

"You're not running a fever or showing any sign of infection, but I'd like to run a blood panel and a PET scan of your brain to be sure."

"A what now?"

"PET. Positron emission tomography."

"Oh, come on," Treyton teased, trying to ease her into one of her eye-catching smiles. "I'm sure the scary needle and the positive... mission...tomato...scan thingy can wait up."

Without responding, Klara turned away and began to make one of the beds that must have been occupied the night before, for the covers were crooked and hanging off to one side. Treyton watched as she unfolded the fresh linen that had been prepared at the foot of the bed by one of her interns, straightening each corner as though stalling for more time. Running her palms over the laid-out sheets, smoothing out any wrinkles in the fabric, she glanced back up at him.

"Do you remember when we were kids and you'd wake up every morning and forget to tidy your quarters? I had to come in and make your bed for eight years."

He reached for her arm and pulled her close enough to him that he could feel the impact of her breath against his chest. A warmth seeped into his heart.

"I took it personally when you stopped coming around," he admitted, tilting her chin up toward him.

Their eyes interlocked, and his skin felt as if it were set on fire. Gravity pulled his arms into a resting position at his sides and, clearing his throat, he turned and began fluffing one of the pillows. The weight of unspoken words compressed the air in the room, and he drank in a series of short breaths.

Once the pillow had been beaten into submission, Treyton cleared his throat, satisfied with the amount of time that had passed and allowed his skin to cool.

He made himself comfortable on the freshly dressed mattress, leaning his back against the wooden headboard. His shoulder blades, protruding from his upper back, protested against the firmness of the wood.

Despite her look of disapproval, seeing as she had just finished changing the linen, she climbed into bed next to him and laid her cheek against his chest. She was small compared to him, like a runt kitten nestled up against its mother's belly for warmth. In her case, however, it seemed to be for comfort.

"Discovering my ability at sixteen made everything difficult," she whispered, surprising him. After their reunion earlier this year, they had agreed that there was no need to address the past or their reasons for growing apart in those years. It didn't matter. What mattered in the present was that they were there for one another. But even still, there was always a small sliver of himself that was curious as to why she had shut him out of her life, refused to talk to him, ignored his calls and text messages, and snuck away any time they had happened to enter the same room without so much as acknowledging the other's being there.

"Reading a book felt like falling from a hundred feet up. I couldn't control all the information in my head, Ton, even when I stopped researching the archives and tried everything in my power to restrict the data that clogged my head. Every touch. Every smell. Every texture. It was too much new information at once."

He sat up, slipping an arm around her shoulders to keep her from slumping into the mattress.

"You never mentioned this before."

And he had a pretty good idea why: their agreement. But as her best friend, he was meant to protect her. She'd been suffering, and he hadn't had a clue about it. What kind of a friend did that make him? Did he want to be the type of friend who made agreements at the cost of his friend's well-being, all so he could have peace of mind about what had gone on during the years that his best friend supposedly wanted nothing to do with him?

"Of course I didn't," Klara spoke through a tense smile before adjusting herself so that she was kneeling next to him, still resting her hand against his chest as his arm fell beside her. "When you're sixteen, you're supposed to be out and having fun. Partying, making friends, not worrying about when your next attack might be or what might set it off. The back of a cereal box when I was eighteen was just as lethal as the barrel of a gun, for God's sake. Everything and anything threatened to hurt me, including you."

There was a crack in her voice. He recognized that crack—a product of anger at the world and one's own self-loathing. There was a rawness in his throat as he swallowed against the urge to cry, unable to meet her gaze.

Desperate to put distance between Klara and himself—between his guilt and her despair—Treyton slid off the bed and readjusted his uniform where it had twisted and wrinkled in places.

"I imagine this story of yours is going somewhere, as they usually do," he said, careful not to let any emotion creep back into his voice. If he so much as hinted at his own guilt for his failure as her friend, she would wish she'd never told him. And there wasn't a thing in the world that he didn't want her to tell him.

In all the years that he had known her, Klara had never been the story-telling type, not unless there was a lesson or higher meaning involved. Every word was methodically chosen.

"My point is," she continued, still kneeling on the hospital bed, "my ability became active two years before my eighteenth birthday. That's early. And there are many cases, too, where abilities develop later than expected."

His brows knitted together as he analyzed her face. There were more cogs turning behind those round eyes of hers. He just couldn't figure out what they meant, or what was forming in her head.

"Have you been tested?" she asked.

Treyton swallowed. "For?"

"The gene."

Squinting at her, he began to see where the conversation was headed. "No."

"If you've inherited the gene, your ability could have developed late." She patted the mattress next to her in invitation.

"Pater is human, and so was my surrogate mother," he reminded her, shooting down the idea altogether.

Her arm sagged when he stayed put, her hand curling into a fist against the bed. "Your surrogate mother also had brown eyes," she fired back, crossing her arms.

A surge of energy rolled over him, igniting his words. "What does that have to do with anything?"

A knot formed in his stomach as a flicker of hurt crossed over Klara's small, childlike face. "It means that you inherited the recessive allele that contained the genetic coding for blue eyes. And recessive genes contribute to more than just eye colour, Ton."

He met her gaze with a fiery blue glare.

"If you inherited a recessive gene for blue eyes from your mother, it's more than possible that, between your parents' crossed genetic coding, you fell within range to inherit the inhumanus gene."

"I vow, in memory of the three founders, all of whom risked their livelihoods to protect the identity of the Resiliens, to pledge the remainder of my existence to ensuring the safety of those we have sworn to protect. Shall I fall before the Ascendancy, I will have honoured my duty and, in return, honour shall befall my name."

"I vow." His voice was shrill with youth.

It was a promise, too heavy a burden for a child's shoulders to bear.

Nevertheless, his vow had been made.

"Just let me do some more tests," Klara said.

Treyton waved a hand in dismissal. "You're not getting a drop of blood out of me unless you pin me down and collect it yourself, Klara," he warned. "Clear me, or I'll clear myself. End of discussion."

She reached for his arm despite the stretch of distance that had formed between them. When her hand fell to dangle at her side, she lowered her head, and her hair fell over her eyes.

Words of ice rolled off of her tongue. "Don't use that tone with me, *Silens*."

Though her opinion was ordinarily valuable to him, he took offence to her speaking to him as though he were a child.

"Sure thing, *Mom*."

Short and not so sweet. The words slipped right off the end of his tongue and into a pool of regret.

Klara's intense glare burned into the surface of his skin as she traced him up and down, as if attempting to identify the man in front of her. He fiddled with the watch on his wrist, growing uncomfortable, before turning his back to her and pretending to analyze one of the medical charts pinned to a bulletin board above one of the infirmary beds.

Quick footsteps caused him to tense his shoulders, anticipating some form of eruption from the small, dark-haired girl. What he got instead were gentle hands placed on his back. An invitation to turn and face her.

"Hear me out, Ton. How long have we been friends?"

A joke similar to, "We're friends, now?" crawled to the end of his tongue, but, reading the sincerity in the hands pressed between his shoulder blades, he decided against it. Sucking in a breath to calm his buzzing nerves, he turned to face her, his movements apprehensive. He was a hostage of silence as his focus rested on the sheen of his boots.

"All these years, and you still can't do basic subtraction."

Treyton's eyes flickered up. When he searched her gaze for any remaining signs of anger, he was surprised to find that it had faded altogether. He moved to wrap his arms around her, hugging her close to his chest with a sigh of relief.

Life was miserable so long as she was mad at him. Freeing himself from the lingering form of his brother's shadow was difficult enough as it was. Klara was one of the few people to treat him as an individual and not just as an extension of James. Of his family.

The same gentle hands that he knew so well pushed back against his chest, forcing space between them both. Klara looked up, her doe-like features hardening.

"I'm not mad at you," she started, clearly noticing his raised brows. "But I am the lead medical practitioner. I can't, in good conscience, let you out into the field without being entirely sure that you're in control of yourself. I can't endanger one of my own."

Heat coagulated in his palms. A burn so intense that he swore he could smell the sour stench of burning flesh. Scorching discomfort threw him to his knees as he balled his hands into fists and buried his head into his lap. Biting back a scream, the bitter taste of blood from where his teeth had torn the skin on his lip nipped at his taste buds.

After thirty seconds, the pain subsided enough that Treyton could lift his head again. Klara knelt next to him with a cotton swab, dabbing an end against his broken lip. Though her brow was furrowed in concentration, he couldn't help but take note of the trembling of her hands.

"You're shaking," he said through laboured breaths, his lungs still trying to recover from the trauma against his body, his hands cramping. His fingers uncurled from the insides of his palms, which were now marked with red. But his skin otherwise remained intact. Unscorched.

Hurrying over to her counter to put the cotton swab into a small, seemingly sterile container, Klara called over her shoulder, "Am not."

Her lab coat swept the floor as she returned to his side in a few strides, her fingers brushing strands of his hair, dampened by sweat, out of his eyes.

"You're not leaving this base until I've figured out what's happening to you."

With a glare of defiance, Treyton rose to his feet. "*Silens* out," he remarked as he turned to leave. He stumbled over himself, his legs dissolving underneath his weight. Holding out his arms in front of him for balance, he shook his head when she edged closer to offer her shoulder. It would be kind of difficult to make a point by storming out when storming out required assistance.

"If I hear from so much as your brother about you leaving this base, I swear to God, I'll have you benched until you're thirty."

The crack in her voice spoke volumes. She meant every single word, and he hadn't a doubt in his mind that she would do just as she'd threatened.

Forcing open the doors of the infirmary with a growl, Treyton refused to look back.

"Don't sprain your tongue," he said finally, pulling the doors closed behind him as he left to stand out in the tunnels alone. There was a weight on his shoulders, and he contemplated succumbing to it and crumpling to the ground.

Treyton slunk down the narrow tunnel that branched away from the infirmary and into the central tunnel. An abrupt force struck his chest as he turned the corner, but when he looked down to see what had hit him, there was only empty space. A painful chill raked over his spine, sending shivers crawling to the tips of his fingers.

Swallowing down the lump of unease that had formed in his throat, he continued forward in search of James, who had to be patrolling the network of tunnels in pursuit of him by now. The impatient troll.

Then, as though he'd been trailing behind Treyton since leaving the infirmary, a dark-haired figure approached him from behind and, eerily calm, James asked, "Have you received clearance?"

"Yessiree," Treyton lied, wearing his best smile as a mask, disguising the guilt that burrowed deeper into his gut. "Just a headache. When we heading out?"

With a satisfied grunt, his brother removed one of the holsters from his belt and forced it into Treyton's hand. As he inspected it, he realized that the holster cradled Treyton's gun.

A jolt of panic brought bile to the back of Treyton's throat. This operation would be more dangerous than anything he'd been a part of before. So much so that James was permitting the use of his condemned choice of weapon.

If something went amiss out there, neither of them would be returning to base later that evening. A stab of something—shame—

reminded him of the conversation he had just had with Klara. If something went wrong, those would be his last words to her.

"Immediately," James barked, shifting his weight between feet and casting a glance over his shoulder.

Was he keeping an eye out for someone or, rather, something?

"We don't have much time. We're heading into the heart of the thing, so we won't be travelling on foot."

FIVE

MILES

"NO," I WHISPERED, covering my mouth with quivering hands.

Crimson painted the streets like a canvas. It was enough to make my stomach roll.

"How?"

The journalist on the screen, an elderly woman with greying roots and unusually clear eyes, frowned into the camera. A series of clips were displayed on the green screen behind her, most of which depicted heartbroken citizens demanding answers in compensation for their losses.

"It appears that compounds One through Four have been infiltrated by a lethal airborne virus undetectable to the Ascendant database. Thus far, zero survivors have been reported. Officials are recognizing this course of events as an act of terrorism led by the Resiliens. We will keep you updated as the facts continue to present themselves."

The broadcast continued in an endless loop, as it would until there were further updates and a new transmission to take its place.

I fell into the back of our couch, my upper lip trembling as I failed to muster the courage to speak. Within minutes—the time in which I had been recording my daily logs—a tenth of the Ascendancy's population had been killed. Tens of thousands of innocent lives now extinguished. And for what? A statement of one's opposing power?

Questions pricked my mind like jagged thorns. How was it possible that this virus, unheard of in history, even existed? Under what conditions had it come into existence? And who exactly was responsible? It was easy to tie the name of a well-known group of rebels to such a merciless crime, but *who* had ordered the deaths of our own? Was it infectious? Could it penetrate specialised equipment meant to protect us? Were there any warning signs or symptoms? Did contact guarantee death?

I rocked my body, holding myself to create a barrier between my internal organs and the impending doom I was allowing myself to imagine. If this was the end, I wouldn't go without a fight. I'd been fighting for well over twenty years. Why would I stop now?

How long do we have left?

"Miles!"

In the midst of my spiralling, I'd had no time to notice Murus kneeling in front of me. He grabbed my shoulders and jerked my body forward.

Despite our most recent disagreement, I threw myself against him, nuzzling my face into the safety of his chest and succumbing to the tears that rimmed my eyelids. With his arms around me, I was shielded from the outside world that was now filled with uncertainty and anguish. Yet, almost as quickly as it had come, his grip on me loosened, and he stood to dismiss himself, leaving me slumped over on the wooden floorboards.

I wiped my nose with the back of my hand. "Where are you going?" I sputtered.

Grabbing his coat from off the back of one of our dining room chairs, he began to rummage through his pockets to unearth his key cards.

"Head Office. The chancellor will be waiting."

I folded my hands in my lap. My legs were numb, bent underneath me. "But it's not safe out there."

His eyes sharpened. "Watch over the base while I'm out," he said with finality, slamming the front door behind him as he left.

I sniffled and wiped the tears from my cheeks, which were blotchy with emotion. I scrambled to my feet and situated myself in front of the display, the pupils of my eyes boring back at me as the screen faded to black.

Thinking that a weak signal was to blame for the interruption in the broadcast, I chewed the inside of my cheek and waited. But after a few seconds, there was still no change.

Puzzled, I went over to check the database register: the Ascendancy's modern-day version of the historical cable box. That device had once displayed television shows, which no longer existed, but these broadcasts weren't meaningless entertainment—they were a way of transmitting information from one source to the general public.

The database register's lights still flickered, indicating that the register was operable, giving no plausible reason for the delay in the broadcast.

"C'mon, you stupid thing," I hissed through my teeth, striking the box with a hesitant hand.

The display lit up again, this time with the transmission of a new broadcast. The format was different from that of the Ascendancy, and the image was incredibly pixelated. It wasn't until I peered closer at the screen that my blood ran cold in my veins, my knees threatening to buckle.

The words, a fragment of my memory, reverberated in my skull: *Shouldn't I be*?

The tips of my fingers traced the edge of the image, my heartbeat weakening as I witnessed the scene unfolding beneath my palms.

Quercus?

In the center of a white room was the same boy I had once known, laid out and strapped to a metal table. I could tell by the faint rise and fall of his chest that his vitals were weak. Whatever illness he had contracted, it was destroying his immune system. His body was failing. If the laboratory technicians didn't euthanize him first, the sickness would soon claim his life.

A creeping sensation caressed my spine. Something told me that I wasn't supposed to be watching this. And yet, I couldn't tear my eyes away from the screen.

"Irrumabo," I mumbled. My knees weakened, and I stumbled backward, catching myself on the coffee table. Bile crawled up into my throat. Where was the feed coming from? Was it live?

Whoever is doing this will rot in a penal institution.

Doing a quick sweep of the base, I was sure to lock and secure every window, peering through each in search of whoever was responsible for the tampered register. I couldn't help but think I was being watched, a pair of transcendental eyes searing marks into the back of my head.

After I had checked every window, my nerves began to settle. *Maybe it's just a glitch in the system,* I attempted to reason with myself. Surely the inhumane footage had been meant for eyes other than my own, if any at all?

The air in the room was chillier than it had been only a minute before. I grabbed my jacket from our coat closet down the main hall, slipping it over my shoulders and drawing it tight around myself. When I returned to the living room, the odd feed had ended. In its place read deep crimson text.

IF YOU WANT TO SAVE HIS LIFE.
OUTSIDE.
NOW.

I grew faint, the contents of my stomach clawing their way up into my esophagus. Stomach acid burned the back of my throat raw. The cold, red lettering blinked, disabling me from turning away even if I wanted to.

Before I had a chance to wrap my head around the meaning of the words, my fingers riffled through my coat pockets in search of my communications device. I had to contact Murus…Didn't I?

I owe nobody. Not Quercus, and especially not you! His cruel tone still boomed in my ears, causing my knuckles to flush white as I tightened my grip on the device. Murus wanted Quercus dead. And if I were an outstanding citizen, I should, too.

I owed Quercus my life, and now his life was in my hands. Murus had made it clear that he did nothing if not for his own gain. And I was nothing if not my father's daughter. This was my decision to make; my life to risk for the sake of a friend.

A friend I had not seen in nearly ten years.

Buckling the belts of my jacket, I rooted about the living room for my key card. It wasn't tucked between the pages of my journal, where I normally replaced it at the end of each day.

Propped up against the wall next to the front door was our shoehorn. I grabbed it, tucking it under my arm, uncertain as to who or what I'd face beyond the security of our base. At least that way I was armed. Kind of.

My heartbeat pounded in my ears as I slipped out the front, easing the door shut behind me with a vigilant hand, careful not to alert my neighbours. If someone were to hear me leaving after the compound-wide curfew, they'd alert Murus to my suspicious behavior, and Quercus wouldn't be the only one whose life was in danger.

As an autumn breeze lapped at the back of my neck, I wrapped my free arm tighter around myself, skipping down my porch steps with alert eyes. The street had been consumed by nightfall, with only the streetlamps illuminating white circles onto the sidewalks on either side of the road. As far as I could see, the street was empty. There wasn't so much as an ambling person returning home after a long, eventful day, or a raccoon rummaging around in someone's hydrangeas, looking for a measly scrap to eat.

The neighbourhood, high-class as its residents were, was neat. The streets were devoid of litter and grime, maintained monthly to ensure that there were no cracks in the asphalt or chips in the curbs.

Silence clung to the air like an unspoken threat, leaving the heaviness of my heightened breathing the only sound within earshot. Stepping further out into the road, the weight of my feet dispersing the gravel, I squeezed my hands into fists, ignoring the pain of my nails digging into my palms.

"Miss Miles Amissa."

My body grew rigid as the voice, unfamiliar to me, alerted me to the added presence on the street. My blood curdled in my veins as I twisted my neck to look in the voice's direction—directly behind me.

No more than ten feet from where I stood loomed two ominous figures. From the shape of their outlines, formed by the silver of moonlight behind them, I made out two gentlemen.

Blinking my eyes, they began to adjust to the darkness, and the men's outlines grew more detailed, no longer shadows amidst the gloom.

Their dark trench coats were embellished with gold-and-white embroidery. They wore black pants that hugged the calves of their legs; their feet were covered by thick, black boots. They both stood still, their hands folded in front of them. Like two statues made of onyx, feet welded to the cement beneath their toes.

Their features were shadowed by the dark, but as I met their eyes, I took a sharp inhale. Their irises were a bold peacock blue that glowed ashen under the persistent street lighting, both inviting and menacing.

Taking a step back into a defensive stance, I jabbed the end of the shoehorn in their direction. "Don't come any closer," I warned, though the tremor in my voice was hardly threatening.

"Careful, James, or she'll remove your shoes," one of them spoke first. He was the taller of the two, and, from what I could make out of his face, younger, too. His movements were fluid as he rubbed his hands together, bouncing on his toes, grinning from ear to ear like an eager toddler.

I narrowed my eyes at them. *James*, I thought, *what an odd name.*

His shorter companion, James, swatted a gloved hand at the back of the first man's head before clearing his throat.

"Forgive my baby brother. It would seem he's misplaced his manners."

"Not that you were wondering, but the name is Trey—*err*—Silens. The grumpy munchkin next to me"—the younger man inclined his head toward the other—"is Currens."

So, his name isn't James? It was curious. It almost sounded as though he were uncertain about their identities, the way he stumbled over the introduction, as though contemplating a silent reminder. Were they withholding information?

I cleared my throat. "Who are you, and which compound do you belong to?"

Amusement glimmered in Silens' radiant eyes. "This one's defective," he said, the words aimed at his brother. "Can I get a new one?"

With a roll of his eyes, his brother took a step in my direction. In response, I withdrew a couple of steps, my eyes locked on them both.

"We do not reside as Ascendant citizens," he answered. He stayed where he was, respecting the space that I had established between us.

Between the unusual black uniforms, the cryptic message on my display, and their haunting presence, a connection forged. The signs that should have spelled it all out for me were now illuminated at the forefront of my mind.

These two men belonged to the same underground movement that had killed thousands. I took another frightened step back, unable to meet their eyes.

"Quercus. Where is he?" I forced the words out before my fear could paralyze my ability to speak, remembering the urgency of Quercus' situation. If it wasn't for what I had seen on the display, I would have run back into my base by now, tucking my metaphorical tail between my legs the moment I'd spotted the two peculiar men. But running and hiding, or making small talk and exchanging pleasantries for the sake of politeness, would only set me back and waste what precious time I had before Quercus would pay for my tardiness with his life. He was dying, and fast.

Silens shoved his hands into his pockets as he turned to his brother with a raised brow. "It appears they're on a first-name basis," he commented. I could see the corners of his mouth quiver with restraint.

As I opened my mouth to object, Currens spoke.

"What does it matter? It will only make our job easier." He dialed something into a small rectangular device, like my communications device, which I hadn't even noticed him pull out.

Curiosity nibbled at the edges of my brain. The technology, unrecognizable to me, must've been developed without the Ascendancy's knowledge.

Muttering annoyance under my breath, mostly at my distractibility, I forced myself to suppress any questions I had until a

further opportunity arose.

"We're wasting time," I reminded them flatly. "And if you plan to waste my time, I'll have no choice but to report your trespassing."

That last part was a lie. If I were to report either of them for their crimes, Murus would be alerted of such a report, and it wouldn't take him long to confront me about leaving the base after hours in the first place. Besides, these two men were the only connection I had to finding Quercus before it was too late.

"Calm your horses," said Silens.

A mischievous smirk tugged at his lips, and my heart jerked.

"Speaking of which..."

SIX

MILES

Motioning for us to follow, Silens broke out into a jog, rounding the base. Panic flared in my gut, my feet feeling as weightless as they ever had as I hurried after him, unwilling to give up my only lead; his brother brought up the rear of our small group. Before I turned the corner after Silens, I shot a glance over my shoulder to ensure that we weren't being followed.

As we broke through the undergrowth that surrounded the rear side of my base, we arrived at a small clearing. Within this clearing awaited what I recognized from my time spent studying the archives to be two equine creatures grazing, shielded by the overhang of trees and shrubbery.

Their shoulders were broad, and their eyes glimmered with an ambition that could only belong to the tamed form of a wild hart. The sheen of their dark coats under the piece of starry sky that peeked through the canopy above us drew me forward, and their gentle nickering encouraged me to stroke their overgrown manes with my free hand, the other still gripping Murus' shoehorn.

"*Equus ferus caballus,*" I recalled from my studies, turning to face the brothers with a look of raw amazement.

"Gesundheit."

As I turned back to the creatures, Silens crept up behind me and whisked the shoehorn out of my hand in one motion, pressing his lips to my ear.

"Wave this around too hard and you might turn into a pumpkin."

The warmth of his breath against my skin made my spine stiffen. I whirled around to face him, my nose inches from his as I proceeded to raise my voice.

"Where's Quercus?"

As I took a step forward to reach for the shoehorn, Silens angled his body away from me, blocking my reach, only to toss the shoehorn as far over my shoulder as he could. Which, given his arm span, was a fair length away. My jaw lingered open as I watched the shoehorn disappear into the bush.

Currens shook his head in disapproval, his posture slumping for only a moment. "Might I remind you, Silens, that we were instructed to bring the girl willingly? I doubt your unpleasantries are at all... favourable."

"I'm plenty favourable, thank you very much." Silens creased his brow.

"Instructed by who?" I looked up at the older brother, unable to hide the insistent curiosity I suspected was scrawled over my expression. Whoever they worked for must have programmed the message and sent it to my database register for me to find. Even if these two halfwits didn't know where Quercus was, their employer surely would.

The thought that followed loomed over me, burdening my shoulders with its weight. The message had been meant for my eyes and my eyes alone. They had known precisely when to intervene with the initial signal, meaning that whoever they worked for had an awareness of my every move. And for all I knew, they still did.

How long have they been watching me?

I took a sharp step back, the curiosity that had gripped me melting away. Suspicion gnawed at my gut and motivated me to reach into my back pocket. Fingers curling around the body of my communications device, my gaze darted back and forth between the two men.

"Who do you work for?" My voice spiked with panic.

Silens and Currens looked between themselves, both of them reluctant to reveal any more about their identities. My fingers tightened, my thumb inching toward the button that would activate an emergency alert for the whole compound.

Silens seemed to follow my motion with his eyes. Holding out a hand, gesturing that I stop whatever it was I was thinking of doing, he spoke with a soft voice. "We'll take you to them."

Vigorously shaking my head, I tried to steady the tremble in my voice. "Why should I believe a word you say?"

Taking another step back, I revealed the communications device to them, my thumb firmly placed on the red button. Alarms began to wail to life from every direction.

"*Irrumabo*!" Silens cursed over the cries of the alarm system.

"We need to disarm the alarms," Currens shouted over the deafening roar, his head turning as he scanned their surroundings in search of the source of the noise.

Unfortunately for them, the alarms were well hidden, even to the registered citizens of the Ascendancy. A sliver of pride brought a coy grin to my lips. The feeling was only momentary, though. The two men had returned to their attention to me, their faces hardened with determination.

The faint scratching of a pencil against my notebook was overcome by the mischievous guffawing of nearby schoolboys. I pulled my nose from the inside of my notebook, its pages scrawled with small doodles, my eyes widening as familiar faces greeted me with their usual crooked smiles.

"If it isn't the compound's token girl!"

Mortem, the eldest of the group and their unofficially designated leader, strolled confidently up next to me with prying, cold eyes.

"What'cha got there?" he asked. His scratchy voice in my ear brought the hairs on my arms to life.

"Nothing," I insisted, hugging the open notebook to my chest. A bad move.

His smile faded.

"Hand it over."

"Please don't." My bottom lip quivered.

Folding his arms, he looked to the others with a crooked brow.

"Do what you want to her."

"You've given us no choice, Miss Amissa. I extend my apologies."

Before I could even try to run, Currens' dark figure rushed forward. Taking my meager wrists in his large hands, he began to haul my small frame toward the equine creatures in spite of my physical protest. I attempted to wriggle out of his grasp, bending my arms every which way, but the effort made no difference. He had the advantage in physical strength.

The tallest of the boys grabbed me by the shoulder, pulling me toward him. I objected, slapping his arm away with one hand. The notebook dangled in my other hand, vulnerable to another boy's grasp as he came up behind me. I turned to him, putting on a brave face, but the menacing look of his twisted grin shattered any bit of confidence I had.

"Fight back," Mortem ordered me, leaning over my shoulder again. "You know you want to."

Shaking my head, rejecting the idea, I took a single step back—into his looming figure. A simple tap; a shoulder to his chest. An insignificant moment of contact followed by significant consequences.

Before I could so much as scream for help, he curled an arm around my head, slapping his hand over my mouth to silence me. His other arm snaked around my waist, pulling me closer to him as he leaned his mouth down to my ear.

"She's all yours, boys."

My eyes widened in horror as his comrades advanced on me. The boy with my notebook still in hand swung his leg up to knee me in the stomach. The wind forced out of me, I couldn't so much as try to wriggle myself free from Mortem's grasp as another boy approached me to grip a clump of my hair. I did the only thing my body allowed me to do at that moment and pleaded with him with my eyes.

If there was so much as a fragment of a kind heart left in his body, I hoped that he would find it in himself to stand up for me.

To help me obtain my freedom.

But my hope died. It should have done so long ago.

Desperate to escape Currens' grasp, I threw up my arms, his own thrown up by extension. Caught in combat with the immense amount of regret that I was about to experience, I hesitated. Then, without warning, I sank my teeth into Currens' exposed forearm. He let out a pain-filled cry, his grasp on me loosening.

This was my moment of opportunity. Swallowing down the gagging sensation as the metallic warmth of blood hit the back of my throat, I jabbed my elbow into his ribcage, buying myself enough time to slip away. The rush of adrenaline that coursed through my veins energized me; I turned and sprinted around the side of the base, making my way for the front door. As I reached for the doorknob, the sound of my heart pounding in my ears was disturbed by Silens' voice calling my name. Ignoring it, I pushed open the door, shut it behind me, and leaned all of my weight against it.

Propping my arms against the wood, I closed my eyes and tried to focus on regaining my breath: sharp inhales followed by shaky

exhales. A burning sensation tore through my side. An aftereffect of the chase.

"Miles, you need to trust us," Silens called from the other side of the door. His weight shifted against it as though he might be able to reach me through the wood somehow.

For a heartbeat, my suspicions faltered.

Perhaps it was his gentle intonation or the mere fact that he was wasting fleeting moments, risking his own capture, to try and reach me even through a closed door…

But without being able to form any explanation as to why, I believed him. Quercus needed me, and despite every lesson about the importance of law and governance that Murus had spent my entire lifetime drilling into me, something told me that I had a different calling.

I put my hand on the doorknob, resting my forehead against the wood as I racked my brain, trying to think rationally. It would only be a matter of minutes before officers arrived, and the strangers would be incarcerated, tried, and then executed when they were found guilty on several counts. If they were innocent, it would be their lives on my conscience. But if they weren't, it was I that would be paying for my poor decision-making skills with my life.

Even knowing this, my doubts were too powerful a force in the foreground of my consciousness. My hand fell away from the doorknob, and I stepped away from the door a few paces, casting an apologetic glance in his direction. If only he could see through the barrier I'd reinforced between us.

"Miles," he continued.

A part of my heart panged a little. What remained of my humanity reached a hand through the bars that I had encaged my heart in.

"Quercus will die without your help."

That little hand inside me recoiled at those words. I was torn between two versions of myself—between the adoptive kin of a highly respected Ascendant citizen and a trembling girl slumped over on the sidewalk.

I wept where I lay on the cold cement. The sky above turned a sickly grey—a sign of a storm fast approaching.

The boys guffawed where they encircled my weakening form, the parts of my scalp where my hair had been torn from my head matting the rest of my dark hair with drying blood. Like a canvas, my body had been decorated with sweltering bruises of purples and yellows. Torn clothes lay next to me, forced from my aching body. Blood, contaminated with dirt and the boys' saliva where they'd spat on me, sure to bring infection and ensure euthanization, trickled from where my skin had been broken by unrestrained beating.

Mortem crouched down in front of me, taking my small chin in his hand and forcing my face up to look at his own. His head tilted to one side as he inspected his work, his coy grin conquering the remaining stretch of his face.

"What did I tell you, boys? Females serve no purpose in our society."

The clearing of someone's throat snapped Mortem's attention elsewhere—behind him. His hand fell to his side, and I, with no strength to hold it up myself, let my head hit the sidewalk with an audible thump.

"Step away from the girl."

I recognized that voice.

I used what little of my strength remained to turn my head, catching a glimpse of the familiar red-locked boy before darkness enveloped me.

I had been only twelve years old the evening of the ambush. And for ten years, up until the targeted broadcast meant for my eyes alone, that had been the last time I'd seen Quercus.

Three days after the beating, when my body had been able to recover enough of its energy to stir awake, I had sat up in bed, Murus observing me from the opposite side of the infirmary room with sunken eyes and a twitching nose. Hoping to thank Quercus, as I could only infer that it had been he who had saved my life that day, I had been disappointed when he'd never so much as visited.

After months of waiting, staking out the Salices' household in search of my saviour, I'd given up hope for a second time.

I owe the Ascendancy nothing, I realized.

But I did owe Quercus my life.

In one fluid movement, I rushed forward and swung open the front door. It slammed against the interior wall, rattling the connecting walls that stretched around me. Greeted by Silens' dimpling cheeks, I took his outstretched hand and followed him at his heels.

SEVEN

CURRENS

WITH A FIRM HAND, he patted the side of Rupedo's neck. Each stroke over the coarse hair more hurried than the last, Currens began to re-evaluate the scenario as it had played out.

He and Silens had been instructed to bring Miss Amissa back consensually. Yet, under the blaring of the alarms system, which still rang persistently through the midnight air, and the knowing intuition of the Ascendant officers growing nearer, he had lost his patience and acted irrationally. And like a small, easily startled mammal, Miles had scurried into the confines of her burrow—a tall standing structure, identical to the others that formed rows on either side of the road.

Rupedo nudged his head against Currens' chest and gave a soft nicker. His dark eyes seemed to trace him in an analytical fashion.

"I'm all right," he assured him, straightening the end of his sleeve and pulling it over the bite wound on his forearm.

He threw his arm over Rupedo's back, leaning into his side as he stared at the back of the Ascendant base, thoughts murky.

Though Currens remembered very little of his upbringing within Ascendant borders, the architecture designed and constructed by the Ascendancy was similar to the architecture that resided in the remnants of his memory.

A wave of nostalgia struck him in the chest, causing his breath to catch in the back of his throat. The indistinct fragrance of rubbing alcohol—used to meticulously clean every building in his mind, including residential dwellings—made the hairs in his nose twinge. Dull silence enveloped him, his last persisting memory from his youth amongst the Ascendancy creeping up on him from all sides.

Clanging. Footsteps. Warmth.

A fog obscured the beginnings of his memory.

Wiggling his fingers, Currens reached up and used his arms to pull himself up over the edge of the table to peer at the meal preparations his father had set down. Glinting metal laid still next to the two rectangular wooden boards, stirring a newfound curiosity only natural for a toddler.

Making a sound somewhere between a grunt and a whine, Currens thrust a pointing finger at the assortment of tools and food objects strewn about.

Pater chuckled, moving around the table to gather him in his arms.

"You want to help, do you?"

Currens nodded too eagerly, butting his head against his father's chin. Whereas Tata would have grown frustrated, frowned, and set him down, Pater only maintained the gleam in his eye.

"You're too young for knives," he said. "Talk to me when you're four."

Crow's feet branched out from the corners of his ageing eyes as he cracked his usual grin.

Mental fog poured in from the edges of his recollection, severing Currens from the remainder of his memory. The lines that had been carved into his father's face by years of experience faded away gradually until the cognitive image had been engulfed by the fog, leaving nothing but a white void in its place.

The sound of shoes hitting the pavement and moving in his direction startled Currens back into a state of awareness. Reaching down and retrieving his dagger from the sheath sewn into the inside of his right pants leg, he sank down to kneel out of sight behind Rupedo.

Silence.

Even the alarms system had shut off, leaving nothing but the sound of rapid, shallow breaths. He rose up to peer over Rupedo's back only to be met by his brother's face, the younger man wearing a proud smirk. Behind him was Miss Amissa, clasping one arm at the elbow. From what Currens could see, she was avoiding his eyes, focusing on the undergrowth behind him.

Paying no mind to the tightness in his chest, he turned his eyes away and returned his dagger to its sheath. He would have to save his apology for a later date, but was sure to make a mental note of it. Clearing his throat and climbing into Rupedo's saddle in a few, fluid movements, he inclined his head to his brother.

"Our time is limited."

"Then we shan't waste anymore of it," Silens replied, mocking his intonation. "How'd you finally get the alarms to shut the hell up?"

Currens raised a brow. "That wasn't you?"

Silens shook his head. "I thought that was you."

Currens shook his head in return, gathering the reins in his calloused hands. "You'll recall that I have no knowledge in electrical intervention."

Silens opened his mouth to reply, but seemed to rethink what it was he was going to say before falling into silence and guiding Miss Amissa over to Emere, who stood restlessly next to her companion, Rupedo.

Watching as Silens instructed Miss Amissa in the practice of mounting a horse, Currens' nerves began to rattle. In the heart of the compound of highest economic status and importance, there was not a single Ascendant citizen or officer in sight. There wasn't so much as a sound to alert them of approaching officers or Ascendant officials. It was as though they had found themselves in a residential area long since abandoned and left to decay—or that would be later rebuilt to accommodate for the Ascendancy's inevitable population growth—the only sign of life residing in the liveliness of a girl they knew very little about.

"We're ready," Silens called. He had climbed into the saddle behind Miss Amissa, his arms curled conscientiously around her as he balanced the reins in front of them. Betraying his embarrassment about being so close to the young woman was the red glow at the tips of his ears and the constant clearing of his throat.

Though they had only just met the young woman, Currens himself couldn't deny that she contained a sort of subtle beauty, despite not any single feature particularly calling for attention. As average as she was, he supposed that the vulnerability she wore plainly on her face held a captivating charm.

The group of five moved at a galloping pace around the edges of the compound, heading further south than Currens imagined Miss Amissa had ever travelled.

As the buildings gave way to an open stretch of landscape, soil newly turned in preparation for undeclared construction on behalf of the Ascendancy, the ball of tension that had burrowed into Currens' chest loosened. Yet he couldn't entirely surrender his suspicions.

After all the errors they had made in retrieving Miss Amissa, they should have faced confrontation with the Ascendancy. And he didn't believe in luck and good fortune.

After an additional twenty minutes of travel, he ordered the group to stop so that Rupedo and Emere could rest and catch their breath.

Rupedo's sides rose and fell rapidly as he fought to regulate his breathing, lowering his head to nose at a patch of grass.

Now that they had passed over the yards of overturned soil, they had reached land that had yellowed and turned to dust under the last of summer's intense rays. Small sections of grass were greener only under shrubbery and tall aspen trees, which provided shade during the daytime; wind gusts, regularly welcomed as a relief against the heat, contained only squalls of hot air.

Despite nature's fiery determination to work against them, Currens failed to feel sweat form on the surface of his brow, a suggestion that he was suffering from severe dehydration. Swiping his tongue over his lips to determine whether or not his mouth was at all dry, he was surprised to find that it wasn't.

"Why have we stopped?" Miss Amissa asked, watching as Silens dismounted from Emere. She seemed ready to jump down from the saddle after him, but Emere protested by swinging herself to the right, startling the young woman into gripping the saddle's horn. Seemingly out of fear that the mare would act unpredictably again, Miss Amissa stayed put.

"Well," Silens said, sitting cross-legged on the ground where the tall grasses surrounding them had been flattened out, "we won't be able to get very far if the horses' hearts explode, now will we?"

"Seriously?"

"Seriously."

Lines formed on Miss Amissa's forehead as she furrowed her brow.

"You don't believe me?"

While the two continued to chat aimlessly, Rupedo and Emere resting under the shelter of a large coniferous tree nearby, Currens wandered further out into the fields on foot, the dry grass crackling underneath his weight.

The need to separate himself from the rest of the group had been lurking behind him since they had begun their journey back to base. Isolation was where he felt most in control, able to predict his own actions and rely solely on his own intuition. When he was the leading head for such groups, as he often was, it wasn't uncommon that things would very quickly spiral out of control due to the unpredictability of other people's actions, usually driven by their own emotional desires. Their time in the heart of the Ascendancy—Miss Amissa's spooking, the alarms system, and the lack of Ascendant officers—was proof enough of that.

Deeper into the fields grew grasses far over his head, and his vision was obscured by the strands of yellow. Using his left hand to pull large sections of the plants away from his face, he ventured further until he found himself standing in a clearing where the foliage had been trimmed to the soil. Bending down to brush at the ground, freshly cut snippings of grass giving way under his touch to form a clump in his palm, a grim realization gripped him. The turf there had been cut recently.

"James!" Silens' panicked voice planted arrows in Currens' heart.

A cold shudder vibrated through his body. Turning, he broke out into a sprint in the direction of the group, the yellow blades like whips against his skin as he used only the sheer force of his body to shoulder his way through the fields. He clenched his jaw, expecting the skin on his face and hands to burn under the violent friction.

Yet the grass felt plush against his skin.

Emerging on the other side of the tall meadow, his eyes locked on the scene that unfolded in front of him.

An Ascendant officer pinned Silens to the ground with a hand to his throat. Several metres from where he scrambled and grasped at the ground around him for leverage laid Silens' gun. It must've been knocked out of his hand when the officers had ambushed the group, giving his brother no time to defend himself before being tackled to the ground.

A few metres away, Rupedo and Emere were tossing their heads and stomping their hooves at the three Ascendant officers trying to advance on them, the officers' focus homed in on Miss Amissa. The young woman stood behind Currens' companions, against the hollow trunk of a tree that had long since expired.

Currens clenched his jaw. They had been outsmarted—ambushed. And though he knew what needed to happen next if they were to escape their current predicament with their heads still connected to their shoulders, he worried that it would further complicate matters.

"Change back!" Currens ordered Rupedo and Emere, exchanging a knowing look with them both.

Raising his voice drew the attention of one Ascendant officer, who left the other two to their own devices to close the space between them.

Before Currens could reach for his dagger, the officer hurled himself at him, the weight of his body knocking him off his feet. Landing on his back with enough force to expel the air from his lungs, Currens tightened his jaw, bracing himself for the flare of pain that would radiate throughout his lower jaw as the officer swung a fist. Knuckles connected with the side of his head.

Yet, once again, the blow never came as anything other than a soft graze against Currens' skin. It was as if the officer hadn't laid a hand on him at all.

Bringing his legs up, Currens kicked as hard as he could against the officer's chest, forcing enough space between them to retrieve his

dagger from its sheath.

When the officer lunged at him again, reaching to pry the dagger from his hand, Currens grabbed him by the collar of his Ascendant uniform. The officer squirmed at first, then thrashed more violently when he realized that Currens had the upper hand.

Squeezing the blade's handle, Currens plunged the weapon into the officer's neck. With a gurgling sound as the blood welled up into his throat, reddened saliva gathering at the corners of his mouth, the officer rolled off of him. He heaved his shoulders as he gasped for air, his body newly deprived of oxygen. It would only be a few minutes before he succumbed to his death, bleeding out into the soil.

Forcing himself to his feet, the warmth of the officer's blood trickling down the length of his arm where he still held the dagger in his grip, Currens turned his attention to the others once again.

Silens had managed to overpower the officer that he'd been tangled with and was now holding him to the ground by the shoulders. Meanwhile, Rupedo and Emere still separated Miss Amissa from the other two officers. By the way they drew back a few paces, Currens could tell that the officers had exploited the last of their patience.

"Put these animals out of their misery," the taller of the two officers ordered. Their comrade reached for their belt.

A gun.

Currens stiffened, his eyes meeting Rupedo's. He held his stare, hoping that alone would startle his travel partner into reaction. There were no words that Currens could offer in time to warn them all about the gun.

His pulse jittered.

The crack of a gun, followed by Miss Amissa's horrified scream, made him want to turn his head away and shield his eyes. Death and suffering were never something that Currens had taken pleasure in, though he had developed a heightened tolerance to the unfortunate elements of reality over his years as an Arxman.

He did not fear death; he feared living.

Currens wrestled with the temptation to avert his eyes, forcing himself to keep his head turned in the direction of the others. If he were to turn away from their suffering, he would be no better than those who were responsible; those at the root of their pain.

A bullet struck Emere. The blood in Currens' veins ran cold at the pain in her cry. With a gaping gunshot wound to her chest, blood trickled off her trembling body and the crimson droplets fell to soak into the earth. Her legs buckled underneath her. She let out a spine-chilling whinny that alerted them all of her suffering—a cry cut short seconds later by the firing of a second bullet.

Currens' throat tightened as he suppressed the urge to wail out. He started toward her. He owed it to Emere to guard her body, at least.

A gloved hand enclosed around his wrist, restricting his forward mobility: Silens, who had managed to render the officer he had restrained earlier unconscious. His brother shook his head.

And he was right. Emere was dead, and to risk his own life before the others were safe would be foolish.

Currens lowered his eyes, unwilling to betray the thoughts behind them. Had they never stopped to rest, and had he never wandered so far off, or been more alert, they would have made it back to the tunnel. All of them, just as alive as they had come.

Emere would still be alive if he had trusted his earlier suspicions, knowing that their escape had been handed to them by the Ascendancy. As her leader and her mentor, Emere had put her life in his hands in faith that he would protect her, even at the cost of his own life. But he had failed her, as well as his own sworn duty to protect the innocent.

As the last signs of life faded from Emere's equine form, the young shapeshifter's body returned to its natural state. She lay facedown, her naked body at the centre of the widening pool of blood, which would be soaked up by the earth.

Rupedo shifted into his own natural form, slumping his body over Emere's, shielding her from the remaining two officers. He wept into the crook of her neck, his shoulders bobbing up and down to the rhythm of his sobs.

"They're inhumans," the shorter officer exclaimed, taking a step back to put distance between themself and the two shapeshifters.

The officer who did not wield the gun—who Currens predicted to be their commanding officer, and could see was a woman now that her body was turned in his direction—grimaced.

Turning her head to glare at Miss Amissa, who had gathered her knees in her arms from her position on the ground, the commanding officer spat, "Terminate the others. I'll grab the girl."

"The hell you will," Silens muttered under his breath next to Currens. He'd retrieved the gun from the holster sewn into his belt and leveled it in the direction of the commanding officer, who was advancing on the Ascendant woman.

The crack of the gun exploded in Currens' ears, firing vibrations through his skull. The bullet tore through the air and embedded itself in the officer's right shoulder. The impact of the bullet sent her lurching backward as she fought the force working against her body, trying to maintain her balance, but she fell onto her back anyway. Blood seeped into the material of her white uniform, turning it a pinkish hue that darkened as the bleeding persisted.

Another crack of a gun split the silence—a shot from the opposing side. From behind the injured officer, her companion had fired a gun in their direction. Clenching his jaw and squeezing shut his eyes, he awaited the tearing of human flesh and the blistering pain that would follow.

One.

Two…

Three…seconds.

Nothing.

They missed?

His body must have gone into shock—a buffer against the sensation of the bullet tearing through his skin. He cracked open his eyes and peered down at his chest, expecting a gory wound where the bullet should have planted itself.

Yet, as he looked down…there was no sign of injury at all.

They *had* missed?

"James…" Silens breathed, pointing to something on the ground. "Look."

EIGHT

CURRENS

FOLLOWING THE PATH OF HIS BROTHER'S FINGER, a prickling sensation crawled along the back of Currens' neck. Between his feet rested the bullet, untainted. Not a fleck of blood marred its metallic body. It reflected the moon's light, making itself known in its bed of yellow.

The officer who had fired the gun lowered his weapon, staring at Currens in bewilderment.

"He's one of them."

Currens' eyes shot open wide and, as if on impulse, he shook his head in disagreement.

That was impossible. His biological parents were citizens of the Ascendancy. Measures were taken to ensure that such an event could not occur. He had even been genetically tested on several occasions since his eighteenth birthday. If he did, by some miracle of human biology, have within his genetic coding the inhumanus gene, it would have been detected at some point within the last eight years.

"Oh, for God's sake," Silens hissed as the officer lifted his weapon to shoot at him again. Lifting his own weapon, he fired two consecutive shots before the officer's finger had even found his trigger. Collapsing at the feet of his comrade, who still held a firm hand against her wound, he was still after a final breath.

Silens whirled on him, knitting his brows.

"Why is it that when I insult you, you get all riled up like a cat around water, yet when a complete stranger waves a gun in your face," he said, prodding at one of the buttons on Currens' uniform coat with a stern finger, "you sit there looking pathetic?"

"You two cannot be serious," Miss Amissa shouted, getting up from her place on the ground and walking over to place herself between him and Silens. Her lips trembled as she spoke. "You both just killed like, what?" She stopped to glance toward the fallen officers. "Four people, and you're bickering. Seriously?"

"In my defence, only two of them are dead." Silens snickered.

Paying his brother no mind, she turned to face Currens instead. "Do you usually have meltdowns when somebody tries to kill you? Because if so, I'm beginning to reconsider our whole agreement."

Agreement? Last he remembered, she had literally put up a fight against coming with them. His arm had the mark to prove it.

Silens' grin cracked wider, and he reached out to ruffle the dark hair on her head. "And what? Go home? I hate to break it to you, princess—"

Unaware that he still had his fingers curled around the hilt of his dagger, it slipped from Currens' grasp. Miss Amissa, having taken it from him in his moment of distraction, pressed the flat edge of its blade to the underside of Silens' chin, making an imprint on his skin.

Silens' Adam's apple bobbed as he swallowed hard, his face tilted to the star-dappled sky, his body rigid.

"Call me that again," Miss Amissa dared.

He held up his hands to vow his compliance, and Miss Amissa withdrew the blade from under his chin. One corner of her mouth twitched as though she were pleased with herself.

But the mood was brief. The reality of their situation seemed to sink in as she turned to examine the clearing. She lifted a hand to her mouth with a breathless gasp.

To Currens' surprise, she looked more confused than she did distraught about the death and pain that had just engulfed them. She seemed to fall into hard thought, running her eyes from person to person, before turning back to them.

"That girl, what is she?" she asked, referring to Emere.

"She was an inhuman," Currens answered simply, careful to hold his tone steady. To not betray the grief that riddled his heart. "On such a high-risk assignment, it was imperative that we had reinforcements in place. Emere—the girl—and Rupedo had the ability to change their physical form to any other living being at their own will. We'd thought that their abilities would give them a low profile and decrease the likelihood of casualties but, as I'm sure you know, the Ascendancy is unpredictable."

His brother wrapped a hand around his elbow, redirecting his attention. "We need to leave before they send others."

Nodding, Currens retrieved his dagger from Miss Amissa's hand and, lifting his leg, slid the dagger back into its protective sheath.

He nodded to the two remaining Ascendant officers. "These two will have too much to tell the next group of officers they dispatch."

"What does that mean?" Miss Amissa asked. But by her expectant look, it was clear that she was only looking for confirmation.

NINE

SILENS

He lingered behind the others as they moved through the dimly lit underground tunnels leading them back home. One of the overhead lights flickered—an indication that, before long, the bulb would burn out and die, leaving the tunnels darker than they'd been before. Like those illuminating the interior tunnels within their base, they washed a sickly blue hue over everything in their vision.

Treyton's muscles jumped at a skittering sound. With round, beady black eyes, a rat appeared from a crack in the cement, navigating its way along the side of the tunnel using its whiskers. Muscle memory had his hand travelling to the holster on his belt, where he had earlier returned his gun. For a split second, the idea of shooting at the rat came to him and, just as quickly, passed.

There'd been more bloodshed than he cared to be the cause for. The two faces of the Ascendant officers forced themselves to the front of his mind.

The way their jaws had dropped when they'd become aware of his standing over them, the muzzle of his gun in line with their heads before they'd turned and tried to claw themselves further from the fate of mortality.

He had killed before. It wasn't a new experience for him, yet with each life he took he was guiltier than he had been before. It was as though he were abusing a power that was not his to abuse. A sign of his humanity, he supposed.

But in a world dominated by the unequal balance of power, sometimes killing was necessary. He had taken their lives in exchange for certainty. For protection. To ensure what remained of his little group's identities was hidden from the rest of the Ascendancy, so as not to put the lives of his friends and family in harm's way.

Closing his eyes, focusing only on his touch against the gun, he chose to believe he was safer in knowing that the weapon was secure on his waist and within arm's reach. It brought a false sense of security. After all, a gun was only as dangerous as its handler. And there were far more dangerous men than him, all handling guns of their own.

Since entering the web of exterior tunnels, it seemed like eyes were scrutinizing the back of his head. Having the gun dampened his suspicions of danger. If a group of Ascendant officers ambushed them again, he would have a better chance of making it out alive with the gun than he would without it.

Ahead of the rest of the group walked Miles and James. Miles, though shorter and without as long a stride, walked with short, hurried steps and was a couple of feet ahead of James despite not knowing the way. She never looked over her shoulder to check if anybody was still following.

Never looked at any of them.

Since discovering the truth about Emere and Rupedo's abilities, she'd been avoiding eye contact and was keeping to herself.

Treyton clenched his jaw. As much as he wanted to scorn her for her prejudice, considering they were inviting her into a place where the inhuman had found a place of refuge, he held a twinge of sympathy for her. She'd been raised by an entire generation of people who had invested all of their fear and misunderstanding into a system that provided them, too, with a false sense of security. It wasn't her fault that the system had led to the unethical murder of thousands of inhumans, as well as those with illnesses and disabilities that were easily cured or manageable, over the last two decades.

Fear of the unknown was what bridled the human race.

When human beings began to evolve, following biology's natural schema, accidents occurred.

People were injured.

They began to question everything they knew about the meaning of life, and everything that a scientific, technological world explained no longer seemed to hold up.

When the government could no longer provide solid answers to the people's abundance of questions, they began to lose their sense of control. And when humans began to lose that sense of control, one of two things happened:

Either they continued to ask questions, knowing there were no definite answers, or they created their own answers.

Wrote their own rules.

Twenty-two years ago, *they* wrote their own rules.

Twenty-two years ago, humanity was split in two.

Amidst a transition that left many grieving, dead, or fleeing their homes, those who were oppressed and deemed subordinate had drawn the sharpest end of a damning double-edged blade.

Euthansia came later, when protests forced the government's hand in instating a newer, less "barbaric" method of elimination.

Miles had been silent for the majority of the trip. Whenever they came to a fork in the tunnels, unsure of which way to go, she would linger in place and watch them to read their body language; to see which way she should go. And when she started in the wrong direction, she would stop and look around, feigning curiosity, as though she were too embarrassed to admit that when it came to their territory, she was powerless.

When she did speak, it was to herself in a hushed tone.

Treyton had been watching her closely. Outside Resiliens borders, she had at least been somewhat predictable—threatening them, stealing away James' knife when his guard fell. He grinned at the memory, almost impressed.

But now, her every move seemed unpredictable. Unstable. Treyton chalked it up to her being uncomfortable or her knowing that she was unfavourably outnumbered.

James, meanwhile, seemed to have no trouble keeping up with her. He, too, remained silent. By some miracle, the bullet had been fired from the barrel of the officer's gun only to ricochet off his brother's chest and fall to rest between his feet. Since, James hadn't uttered a word. He hadn't so much as brought up the subject to question the logistics—to pick Treyton's brain about what he had, or hadn't, seen.

It was unusual, even for him, to not try to pick something apart and make sense of it.

Treyton pondered, running a hand over his shirt where the bullet should have implanted itself in his brother's chest.

Though the anthene textile all of the Resiliens' clothing and uniforms were constructed from was resistant and "bulletproof," the fabric was thin, so a bullet fired from close range should have been impossible for the material to withstand. He contemplated pulling his brother aside to bring up the matter. But if he did, he worried that his own suspicions about his mysterious "illness" would bleed through the meaning of his words.

Shutting his eyes and slowing his pace, the distance between him and the others stretching further, he tried to focus. To bring about whatever it was that he had experienced earlier that day in the conference room and in Klara's infirmary. But without knowing what it *was* he was trying to call on—assuming that he wasn't ordinarily human, as Klara had suggested—it was no use.

Her face appeared to him in his head, and he was reminded of the hurt in her eyes when he had defied her. He remembered the way that she could barely steady her voice as she had threatened to report him for walking away in his "condition."

Stuffing his hands into his pockets, Treyton tried to fight the sinking feeling in his stomach. Once they returned home, the four of them would have to be admitted to her wing for medical clearance—standard protocol after returning from assignment outside the tunnels. He wasn't sure that he could face her after the way he had stormed out, defying her professional orders as well as dismissing her personal sentiments.

A chilling thought forced itself on him. What if Klara had discovered that he had gone without her medical approval and, by some twist of fate, had followed them in order to keep an eye on him? It wasn't an uncommon practice for medics who suspected that something might be off about an Arxman's well-being but lacked the medical evidence required to withhold them from duty. It could have been her shot dead rather than Emere. The image flickered into his mind—her arms tangled underneath her, her corpse still, and her lifeless eyes pointed in his direction. Then, almost as fast as it had come, the image faded away.

Treyton shook his head, forcing the visual away. *That's a tad extreme,* he thought, scolding himself for even thinking it in the first place.

Reality was beginning to sink in.

Emere would not be returning home.

Rupedo had pleaded with James and him, insisting on carrying Emere's body. But her added weight would have only set them further back, putting them at risk for another attack. Another weight—the weight of leaving her behind, unable to be buried ceremoniously by her loved ones—now rested on their shoulders.

Head hanging, his chin tucked into his chest, Rupedo walked only a few feet ahead of Treyton. The soles of his bare feet scraped against the cement as he dragged them onward.

When Treyton had approached Rupedo, still slumped against Emere's body, his skin and hair had been matted with her drying blood. In fact, the boy even now made no attempt to smooth back his hair, the blond edges dangling over his face. He had given him his jacket to cover his naked body so that he might find a spark of what remained of his self-respect, the jacket hardly long enough to reach his wobbling knees.

Treyton cursed himself silently, wishing now that he had made the effort to bring Emere home himself. To try and at least move her body somewhere that wasn't so out in the open, likely to be retrieved by Ascendant officers and incinerated. But he knew, even if he had, his brother would have intervened to protest. Not that he usually listened to what his brother had to say, but they had run into enough trouble as it was. He hadn't a doubt in his mind that they would be hearing the worst of it once they were standing before their fathers and being asked to report the day's misfortunes.

After what seemed like hours, but was likely only ten minutes of walking in mind-numbing silence, the group reached the towering, locked doors that separated the Resiliens' hidden underground base from the outside world. Lights on either side of the doors, a blinding red, blinked, signalling that the locks were still in place and security systems were in order.

James approached the reinforced steel, inserting one half of his key card into a small machine that protruded from the right-hand side of the doors—a component of the lock's electrical circuit. The machine swallowed the remaining half of the key card, taking a few seconds to process the information stored, before spitting it out.

After retrieving it from the machine, the doors began to open, a soft *whirr* bouncing off the tunnel walls. As the steel slabs parted to reveal the beginnings of the interior network of tunneling, a vibration in the ground crawled up from the soles of Treyton's shoes and into his knees.

That main tunnel, ten feet wide and arching sixteen feet above their heads, was a central line that ran in every part their hidden world, through to numerous other tunnels, each leading to a different sector: residential, medical, security, and external affairs, just to name a few. Only small, rectangular signs bolted to the cement walls where the main tunnel branched off into different departments provided direction.

Those born within the confines of those cement walls, like himself, or raised within them at a young age, like James, knew the tunnels by heart and could sketch their paths from memory on a piece of paper.

"Welcome home, boys."

Lieutenant General Alessandra stood over the threshold of the now-parted doors. Though she seemed to be directing her words at him and James, it was clear by the distrust in her tone and the way she glared at Miles out of the corner of her eye that her suspicions about the newcomer—a citizen of the Ascendancy, after all—were heightened.

Miles, who took notice of the hostility in Alessandra's demeanor, which she made no attempt to hide, shuffled closer to Rupedo and tilted her head upward to avert her eyes.

The sight of Rupedo, his body cloaked only by Treyton's coat, his face flecked with dry blood and his eyes red from crying, drew Alessandra closer toward the group. She peered in between the four of them and over their shoulders, searching.

For Emere, no doubt.

When it became clear to her that there was nobody else accompanying them, she frowned. "I see."

"I assume my father sent you to escort us?" James asked, straightening his shoulders.

What a kiss-ass, Treyton thought.

Rupedo gave a sudden sob, wrapping his arms tighter around himself.

Treyton's heart ached for him. The boy, only sixteen, was trying to contain himself, both physically and emotionally. But grief was an experience that broke any barrier raised up against it.

It hadn't been long ago that Treyton was sixteen and experiencing grief for the first time. Every bone in his body had threatened to snap in two if someone looked at him the wrong way. His heart had felt as though it were dying cell by cell.

"You'll be hearing more from me later, but I do expect a full report from you," Alessandra answered, eyes pointed at James, softening her voice in consideration of Rupedo.

James nodded. With that, Alessandra and the four Arxmen accompanying her began to make their way back into the central tunnel. They made it a few paces before Alessandra stopped, turning her head to call over her shoulder, "You must consult with the medical wing!"

At the mention of the medical wing, mixed with her earlier mention of his fathers, a wave of lightheadedness sent Treyton reeling. Klara had threatened to contact James if he left base without her sign-off, but, seeing as he had been out in the field alongside James, he wondered if she might go as far as to bring the issue up with their fathers.

If it wasn't for the way they had left things between them, she would have kept quiet if it meant protecting him from Tata's wicked temper. But after his outburst, he couldn't put it past her to betray his trust to spite him for how he had acted.

James shouldered past Treyton as he hesitated to draw further into the tunnel. "Could you focus?" he hissed.

Clearing his throat, Treyton bounced forward to walk next to him. "Have you gotten any texts?" he asked.

"Pardon me?"

"On your phone," Treyton clarified. Not that it should have required clarification.

James reached into his pocket, retrieving the phone and holding it up without looking at him. "You mean my communications device?" he asked.

Gritting his teeth, Treyton resisted the urge to roll his eyes, knowing that it would only elicit an unwanted lecture from his brother about self-respect and poor communications skills. And that would be coming from a man who was practically an android—set shoulders, a straight mouth, and glassy eyes devoid of any emotion other than authoritativeness.

If authoritativeness were an emotion, that was.

They'd had this exact conversation about the device a million times before. It was just like James to be so formal about everything, even with something as simple and mundane as a phone. The back and forth, trying to have a normal conversation with him, had become exhausting. After hours of trying to get him to break out of his unbearably robotic way of describing the world around him, the two of them hardly spoke beyond professional necessity.

"You know damn well what I meant."

James looked hard at him. "Tread lightly," he warned, his eyes darkening.

Treyton took a breath. He wasn't going to get the information he wanted if he instigated a fight first.

"I'm sorry," he said, swallowing bile against the words deprived of any real meaning. "On your *communications device*."

"I have not received any correspondence," James answered, his gaze focused on the walk ahead.

Despite how irritating it was that he was compelled to use a term like *correspondence*, some of the weight on Treyton's shoulders rolled away. Neither Pater nor Tata had tried to contact them while they were out in the field. By extension, it meant that Klara had kept quiet about the events of that morning. His condition was still a private matter.

Unless, of course, Klara had been too busy with her duties since he had left that morning, meaning that the topic could still come up in conversation if he didn't address it with her in person first.

"Hey."

Something brushed against Treyton's wrist. He slowed his pace and peered down at Miles, who had fallen into step next to him. Her face was contorted with something resembling conflict or concern. With her fingers still lingering against his skin, she asked, "Are you okay?"

"Okay?" he echoed, his eyes trailing to where her fingers rested against his arm. He lifted the same hand to scratch the back of his head, breaking away from her touch without making the action noticeable. Though she seemed of no real harm, she *had* put a knife to him. "Yeah, I'm okay. It's just been a…rough day, y'know?"

Miles nodded, letting her gaze fall to her feet, and Treyton watched her. He hadn't initially thought her to be the caring type, given how she had threatened to slit his throat and all only two hours ago. Then again, his assessment of her was based primarily on what she wasn't saying, rather than what she was.

As they turned down the passage that branched into the medical wing, Treyton was startled by the lineup of Arxmen outside.

Out of the corner of his eye, he watched Miles inch closer to him, her black eyes homed in on the Arxmen.

Suspicions were high because of her connection to Murus Amissa, which Treyton understood. Bringing her into their self-proclaimed safe haven was a risk that endangered the lives of thousands of innocents. Even still, he understood what it was like to be vulnerable in a foreign place, alone despite being surrounded by people—people you weren't sure you could rely on, but hoped to God for your own sake that you could. His eyes wandered to his brother, and his heart jerked.

Most of the Arxmen regarded him with a curt nod as they passed the lineup. One man in particular, however, who stood closest to the infirmary door, had angled his body away from the group.

Treyton narrowed his eyes.

Is he trying to hide his face?

As they passed through the doors of the infirmary, he tried to catch a glimpse of the Arxman's face. The only distinct feature he managed to pinpoint before disappearing behind the cement wall was a white scar that ran from the bottom of his lower lip to the tip of his chin.

TEN

SILENS

NO MORE THAN A FEW SECONDS INSIDE THE INFIRMARY, Treyton's eyes began to wander in search of Klara. The beds lining the walls on either side, normally separated by sheet dividers when occupied by the ill and injured, were entirely empty. The back of the long room where Klara usually stood over the computer on the counter, logging her medical records and greeting patients as they came and went, was vacant as well.

His eyes found their way to the door that read *MEDICAL PERSONNEL ONLY.* She'd probably ducked in behind that door, an entrance he had never had clearance to enter no matter how persistently he had pestered her about it. Probably to refill a prescription or write a medical journal entry about a recent discovery she'd made about his apparently recessive gene.

Whatever that was, Treyton still wasn't certain.

The door squeaked as it swung inward, and he held his breath. Just as he had suspected, she'd been in the back room. Doing what, he couldn't be sure.

Poking her head out from behind the door, the rest of her body following suit, she balanced three large cardboard boxes, failing to notice their arrival. He thought to offer her his assistance, but decided it best to stay quiet. Large objects made good projectiles.

Setting the boxes down with a *thud* on the counter, she retrieved her clipboard from where it rested against her computer.

"Oh my God, what happened?" she asked, her attention drawn to Rupedo as she tucked her clipboard under her arm, concern illuminating her mottled brown-and-green eyes.

James opened his mouth to explain, but Treyton cut in before he could stop himself. A habit to break another time, he decided.

"We were ambushed."

Klara's lip twitched as her gaze burned into his. "Oh dear," she said coolly, turning her back to him as she began to examine Rupedo.

Miles leaned toward him to ask under her breath, "What's her problem?"

Whisking a tissue from a nearby tissue box and twisting it around his finger to keep himself occupied, Treyton found that the thickening of the surrounding air made it difficult to breathe.

"Somebody put raisins in her cereal."

He didn't bother to explain that it was *he* who was Klara's problem. She'd have follow-up questions, questions that he wasn't particularly in the mood to answer for the time being. Or at all, if he was honest with himself. Especially not in the presence of someone he had only just met hours ago, and not even on his own terms.

Klara guided Rupedo to one of the beds, handing him a medical gown that she'd pulled out from one of the dresser drawers up against the wall. After pulling the curtain around to give Rupedo some privacy as he changed, she walked back toward their group to stand in front of Miles.

"It's refreshing to see a new face," she said, holding out a gloved hand for the Ascendant woman to shake.

Miles surveyed her hand, catching Treyton's eyes and casting him a look as though to ask, *Can I trust her?* When he shrugged his shoulders, deciding it best if she interacted with other civilians of her own accord, she took Klara's hand in her own and gave it two firm shakes.

"Miles, right?"

"How do you know who I am?" asked Miles, cocking her head to the right as she allowed her hand to fall away.

A grin tugged at Klara's lips. Treyton watched as her face lit up, trying to swallow down the lump that had formed in his throat over the hours like a benign tumour. Not a death sentence, but unwelcome all the same.

For as long as he had known Klara, she'd never been unkind to a human soul. Even patients who were under an immense amount of stress—because they had been diagnosed with a chronic illness or were recovering from a painful injury for months at a time—who would threaten her or speak harshly to her were always greeted with a smile and given her best. If altruistic morality had a mascot, she would be a surefire choice.

The first time he had seen her brazenly angry was that morning. He wished he could reverse time and take back the way he had acted. Anything to have her smile at him that way again.

"You've become a household name around here," Klara explained. "I can guarantee you that there isn't a person around here who doesn't know who you are."

"Oh." There was a flush of red to Miles's cheeks. "And you are?"

Klara waved James over, walking him to one of the beds and instructing him to take a seat, despite his look of disapproval.

"You can call me Klara. I'm the head of medicinal practices and genetic research."

"I am perfectly healthy, Miss Davis," James assured her, refusing to sit on the bed's edge despite her insistent hand against his chest.

Taking up her clipboard and a pen from her chest pocket and

pressing its tip to the notepad, she shot him a look that emanated superiority.

After he cleared his throat and sat down as he'd been told, Klara began a standard examination. Ears, nose, throat, the works.

Treyton had folded the tissue into a tiny square and squeezed it between his thumb and forefinger like a tiny sandwich.

"How long is this going to take?" he asked, only afterward realizing that he had spoken in a tone harsher than he'd intended when he caught Klara's fiery stare. Her mouth was pinched tight, her forehead creasing as she wrinkled her brow. He had never been more caught off guard than in that moment, and less than an hour ago he'd been charged by an Ascendant patrol. Averting his eyes, he stared down at the tissue in his hands, unfolding it restlessly.

When Klara replied, there was a hard edge to her voice that made him flinch. "As long as it needs to, Mr. Venus."

Ouch.

The edge in her voice softened when she spoke to James. Treyton suppressed the urge to sneer.

"Are you in any pain?"

"No," James answered.

Klara lifted the bottom of his shirt as she searched for any signs of bruising, and James jerked away from her.

After a soothing "*Shh,*" Klara was able to continue her inspection. When she was satisfied, she nodded and hopped up to sit on the bed next to James, scribbling something down on her notepad.

"I'm going to keep Rupedo here for the next few days for psychological evaluation," she said, casting a glance in the teenager's direction. "If he doesn't show signs of improvement, I'll have to run a central line to administer his medication and fluids. But, as far as I can see, you're free to go, James."

"Thank you kindly." James hopped down from the edge of the bed, pulling the edge of his shirt down around his waist. "And I mean in no way to interfere with your work, but we've been ordered to report back to my fathers as soon as rationally possible."

Klara nodded, setting her clipboard down next to her. "Duty calls, right?" she said, leaning forward to rest her hands on both knees. "I'll make these next couple of examinations quick."

Once again, she smiled. Treyton gritted his teeth, wishing that she would knock it off with all the smiling. At this rate, the guilt was sure to swallow him whole.

"Well, Miles, how are you feeling? Any bruises or minor cuts that I should check? I need to be sure that I log everything accurately so that I can submit my official report." Klara glanced over at the clipboard resting next to her, as though already writing notes in her mind that she would later transcribe to paper.

"I feel okay," Miles answered, looking down at herself as though an injury, if it existed, would call out and make itself known. "Just a little confused, I guess."

Klara cracked a grin, reaching up to tuck a strand of her hair that had gone astray behind her ear. "I can see how all of this might be hard to work out at first. If you have any questions, consider me your walking FAQ page."

"My what?"

"FAQ. Frequently asked questions. If you've got a question, chances are I have an answer for ya. I'll have to run a full series of tests later but, at least for right now, you're free to go."

ELEVEN

MILES

FREE TO GO. I clamped my lips together, fighting off any sure signs of amusement. Was it because they rejected the Ascendant standard that they spoke without reservation? Or was it because they didn't care? Their words held no meaning. Carried no weight.

When one thought of what it meant to be free, it was a suggestion of being able to do, say, and think without fear. To act according to one's own principles. But with the rules, regulations, and expectations put in place by the Ascendancy, this freedom was only an ideal. Some thought to realize freedom through compliance. Others, through political power or research-based achievement.

But I knew better.

Freedom was a myth meant to instill motivation into those of us under the control of a central power. Our actions, words and thoughts weren't our own.

Free to go.

My eyes darted around the room—at the near-strangers, save for what I knew of their names or rankings.

At the infirmary walls.

Where did I have to go?

In a whirl of emotions, driven by my own selfish desires, I had turned my back on the Ascendancy.

On my home.

On my father.

And, in many ways, on myself.

I'd abandoned it all with no regard for my own safety or what would happen to me. I hadn't forgotten that in that very moment, surrounded by concrete and steel, *I* was the enemy.

If my suspicions were true—if I was amongst members of the Resiliens—there would be no returning home. There was a target pinned to my back, between the blades of my shoulders. And after the fallout of that morning's massacre…

Currens turned to Silens and said, "Miss Amissa and I will go ahead. Join us when Miss Davis has completed her examination."

Dipping his head to Klara, who only stood and grinned in response, Currens marched toward the exit.

"Why don't we wait for her to finish?" I asked, remembering our earlier scuffle and glancing between the brothers as the distance between them stretched wider. I didn't move either way, reluctant to be left alone with the eldest brother, yet also unwilling to defy him.

From what I'd learned about Currens thus far, he behaved like a piece of complex machinery. Like he had a voice in his ear, dictating his every action. At the very least, I could read Silens; his actions had precursors. Currens was reminiscent of a being of artificial intelligence. Only I lacked knowledge of his algorithm, making him a foreign entity.

A threat until further notice.

Currens held my gaze, and my heart jerked in my chest. I thought he might rush toward me and seize hold of me again, only to remove me from the room by force. But all he gave was a dejected sigh as he propped himself against the wall.

Klara cleared her throat, her expression blank. "Well, all right then. Sit down, Ton."

Silens' lips parted at this. Complying, he sat on the medical bed. Klara proceeded to give him a quick examination, using her fingers to check for bruising. Then she reached into her coat pocket and retrieved a flat, elongated device.

"So, about that ambush?" She lifted her head, turning her attention toward the younger of the brothers rather than her work.

"We let our guard down," Silens answered, his eyes darting to glare at Currens, who remained silent. "They were waiting for us only about thirty minutes out from the entrance to the tunnels."

Klara, who was running the device down along the length of Silens' arms, stiffened and stopped what she was doing. "That's too close. Do you think…?" Her words tapered off.

"That they knew where to look?" he continued for her, following up with a nod of his head.

Klara held the device up to read the text that blinked across its small, rectangular display. "Or you were followed," she said, not looking up from the display's contents. Concentration carved lines into her mouth.

"A spot in the grass was trimmed to the earth," Currens cut in, still leaning a shoulder into the wall, crossing a foot over the other. "I suspect that they'd set up a stakeout long before we arrived in the vicinity."

"So they were just as surprised to see you as you were them," Klara mumbled, half to herself.

Slipping the device back into her pocket, Klara once again picked up her clipboard and began to scrawl notes onto the sheets of paper. I watched her fingers as they wrote. She was quick, the tip of her pen never leaving the page until she'd finished her thought and set the clipboard aside once more.

I imagined her notes were incomprehensible. Wouldn't it be easier, both for the sake of organization and accessibility, to record her notes electronically, or at least as a vocal recording?

Keeping physical files was an old method, used primarily in the twenty-first century. While useful for keeping one's thoughts and observations in order, flipping through sheets of paper consumed too much precious time, not to mention too much space. And paper was a weak material, vulnerable to the elements of nature should a disaster occur.

"Now, under normal protocol I would keep you all here and run mandated tests," Klara said, running a finger along a line of text written on her clipboard. "But I'm afraid we just don't have the time right now. I'll have to schedule the three of you specific appointments for early tomorrow morning."

"What kind of tests?" I asked.

Given what I'd seen of Klara's preference for methods outdated by several hundreds of years, I wouldn't have been surprised if she'd also had a knack for electrodes or 14-gauge needles.

My skin crawled at the thought of the needle's puncture extracting my bodily fluids, which I would have preferred to remain within my person.

The sight of my blood had always been enough to make me woozy. When I was ten or eleven years of age, I'd awoken to the feeling of warmth seeping across my chest. When I'd sat up in bed, I'd discovered that blood was dripping from the tip of my nose and soaking the fabric of my nightshirt. I remembered being lightheaded and disoriented, and the amount of blood had only worsened things.

That night, I'd fallen unconscious and awakened in my compound's medical centre, greeted by several medical technicians that my father had ordered to watch me overnight. My father, meanwhile, had been nowhere to be seen. Not until three sunrises later. That same night I'd passed out, he'd taken a last-minute flight out to Compound 34 to attend several meetings pertaining to work.

The corner's of Klara's lips curled upward into a small smile. "Nothing too crazy," she answered. "I wouldn't lose too much sleep over it. I've tested these two hundreds of times."

My gaze darted between the two brothers, who hadn't moved an inch.

Silens' head snapped in my direction, his eyes wide. I scratched at the back of my wrist with the opposite hand, recoiling under his wild gaze.

"This woman"—he jutted a finger toward Klara—"is a madman. Have you ever felt every bone in your body splintering into thousands of fragments?"

Without flinching, Klara slapped the back of Silens' head with her clipboard. There was a *thwack* as the wood met his skull, and the unsuspecting Silens rocked forward, cradling the back of his head with both hands.

"What the hell was *that* for?!"

"*This woman* is about to throw you out of her wing!" Klara hissed through her teeth. "You two, strange men, brought a confused young woman here," she said, throwing her hands up and rotating on her heels once to gesture to their surroundings. "Don't you think that's scary enough without you two airheads frightening her with threats of splintering bones?"

Currens stood up straight, eyes wide with disbelief, as if to say, *What did I do?* Silens, meanwhile, stared hard at Klara. Hands gripping his knees, his knuckles bleached.

Whatever it is the two of them are fighting through, I thought, *Silens must be stomping on thin ice.*

In the thirty seconds that followed, the room was silent. Not a single person uttered a word, afraid to say something that might cause another outburst. The only sound I could hear was the thrumming of my own heart in my ears.

Trying to calm my buzzing nerves, I took slow, deep breaths. I had to admit, I was terrified. These people were strangers to me, and yet I'd decided to follow them here. A place where everybody was on edge because of my presence. Nothing and everything was frightening.

Though Currens had been somewhat cool toward me, barely acknowledging me if he could help it, neither of the two young men had acted hostilely toward me. Around them, it became easy to forget that I was in foreign territory with dozens of pairs of eyes turned toward me. Not that I was going to let my guard fall just yet.

"We need to leave," Currens snapped finally, his words slicing through the tension like a hot knife as he approached Silens, who was still seated on the medical bed.

Wrapping his hand around his brother's arm, he forced him to his feet. "My sincerest apologies for our disturbance."

Still holding Silens' arm, he marched toward the exit without another word.

I exchanged a look with Klara, whose lips were taut with an apology. Then, before Currens could call after me or get frustrated about my loitering behind, I lolloped after the brothers.

As I followed them out the door and back into the tunnels, the watchful gaze of the men lined up outside reminded me of my position—a pawn in a game on a mass scale. Only I'd found myself on the wrong end of the playing board.

Keeping my chin tucked to my chest and my eyes focused on the cement beneath my feet, I lingered close behind the brothers. I left only enough space between us so that I was close enough to feel somewhat secure, yet not so close as to trip over their heels.

We turned down another narrow tunnel and entered a room much smaller than Klara's, which lacked the infirmary's abundance of furnishings. In the centre of the room stood a long table, the edges worn—a sign of age and years of use. Chairs with tall backs surrounded the table. Their arms were engraved with symbols that I couldn't make out.

"I'm glad to see you both safe and sound," a silvery voice said. Allowing my eyes to travel up from my feet, I took notice of the two men sitting at the end of the table furthest from where I stood. My heart leapt into my throat, disabling my ability to breathe as my eyes fell on one of the two men in particular.

The graying hair, broad shoulders, and aging eyes.

I blinked again, the figure's resemblance haunting.

Murus?

TWELVE

MILES

SHUFFLING THROUGH AN ARRAY of what appeared to be file folders laid out on the table, the man paid our arrival no mind. The man sitting next to him, meanwhile, leaned back into his chair and greeted us with an open-mouthed smile. A row of men, dressed in dark uniforms similar to those lined up outside, leaned their backs against the wall opposite the entrance.

Squinting my eyes, I tried to get a better look at the disinterested man's face. Confusion bogged my mind as I tried to decipher the image before me. The Murus I knew would never go out of his way for my well-being, never mind enter enemy territory without armed forces to execute the lives of all those residing within these tunnels.

My heart jerked in my chest. Nobody within the Ascendancy had been able to so much as locate the residence of the Resiliens, yet there I was standing in its heart.

Alone.

Even if Murus by some miracle wanted to come to my aid, he would have no idea where to look. By sunrise, any search that might be conducted would draw to a fruitless conclusion.

I wasn't a commodity that Murus would be eager to unearth.

"Don't you go befriending them like you always do," the man resembling Murus snapped. He wasn't Murus, I realized, as he glanced up from his files to regard us all with a tepid look. My shoulders relaxed.

Murus' gaze would have melted the skin off my body with a grimace alone.

"Like I always do? What on earth does that mean?" the man next to him answered, his smile still plastered to his face.

It was beginning to creep me out, frankly. Nobody was *that* happy.

The Murus lookalike—Scowling Man, I'd decided to call him—snapped his head around to glare at his peer.

"You know very well what I mean." He'd paused his shuffling through the files, rubbing his fingers together.

The smile faded from the other man's face. "Not in front of the kids."

Scowling Man ran a hand through his greying hair. "They're grown men, not children."

My stomach twisted into a knot, bile rising to settle in the back of my throat. The dynamic was familiar. The heavy-hearted sighs; the bickering; the hard, drawn-out stares that pierced my heart; the long-awaited outbursts.

In the months leading up to my dad's euthanization, I'd integrated these disputes between my dad and Murus into my daily routine. Leaving before the sun stirred the rest of my compound awake, I had written in my journal, returning only as my dad set our evening meal out on the dining room table.

Silens' eyes caught mine. They were lucid with anger, but softened under my watchful gaze. I experienced a pang of sympathy for him, and wondered if he'd become just as accustomed to the sharp words and unresolved venom as I had.

"Can't I be glad that our children are safe?" the man I assumed to be Scowling Man's husband asked with a frown.

So Currens and Silens are their sons, I thought. Their relation to Currens made sense, but Silens seemed misplaced somehow.

Now Scowling Man was leaning forward and jabbing a finger in his husband's face, as if to accuse him.

"They went and shit all over the plan, Pater. So put away your I'm-so-glads for *once* and admit that your *boys* screwed up."

"They're *our* boys," Pater said incredulously, the corner of his lip twitching.

He's beginning to lose his composure, I realized. I wondered how much more he could endure before his optimistic exterior cracked.

"They are Arxmen first and our boys second. As far as I'm concerned, the two men standing in front of us ought to be disciplined for the way they've behaved."

An itch formed in the back of my throat, and I swallowed hard to keep from coughing.

What behavior are they even talking about? What are Arxmen?

"Your children came home with their heads attached, Tata," Pater replied, his voice brittle. "You could at least try to be grateful for that."

"Would you two knock it off already?" Silens interjected, his words erupting.

Stalking toward the table, he leaned in toward them with both palms placed flat against the table's surface. "We brought you the girl like you asked."

My face contorted, but I pressed my tongue to the roof of my mouth to keep myself quiet. To speak to his parents in such a sharp tone was a daring move.

The thought of interrupting the hostilities of the conversation crossed my mind, only so that I might steer the discussion in a way that pertained more to the answers I needed. I'd come in search of

Quercus, yet I'd been caught in a web of something grander. Though I didn't have a handle on almost anything that was going on, I was sure of one thing: I wasn't there to get involved in their familial troubles.

Scowling Man, or Tata as they called him, threw himself back, straightening against the spine of his chair. "Please," he said, gesturing to the open seats. "Sit and stay a while. We have *plenty* to discuss."

My eyes followed Currens as he moved around the table, seating himself next to Tata. As he straightened up against the back of his chair, I realized that he was shorter than both of his fathers.

Half expecting Silens to sit next to Pater, I was surprised when he shifted a few footsteps closer to them only to remain standing, folding his arms. I considered joining him, but thought better of acting even the slightest bit defiantly when I'd only just arrived. And given the tension already hanging thick in the air, I did not want to be a catalyst in a situation where an explosion seemed imminent.

"Sit anywhere you'd like," Pater urged.

Bumps formed along the lengths of my arms, alerting me that their gazes were all fixed on me. Wandering to the end of the table opposite them, I sat, placing as much distance between myself and *the other* as I could. My shoulders were up to my ears as I slumped forward, my spine curving.

"My name is Pater Venus," the softer man said. "And this"—he inclined his head toward Scowling Man—"is my husband, Tata Venus."

Venus.

An Ascendant surname.

I regarded them both with stifled curiosity, my shoulders drooping as the tension melted from them.

Despite them being complete strangers with intentions I couldn't even begin to theorize about, the newfound knowledge of their surname made them the slightest bit less intimidating. In a room brimming with uncertainty, this was my first glimpse at fellowship. A way to connect, to reach them despite the barrier of opposition standing between my people and theirs.

If I treated them just as I would treat fellow citizens of the Ascendancy, with poise and formality, I wondered if I might gain their trust.

"Thank you for hosting me," I said, straightening up to sit taller.

Pater smirked. "I'm sure you must be a little confused about what exactly is going on here."

"A lot confused, actually."

The wood of Tata's chair squealed as he rocked forward, folding his hands over the top of his scattered files.

"Allow me to explain, then," he said.

His husband lent him a look of warning, but did not dare interrupt.

"To put it simply, your arrival here signifies the beginning stages of the Res Novae."

"The Res Novae," I echoed, the words rolling off my tongue with ease. The words were natural to me, as though I had spoken them my entire life. "Political revolution?"

"Precisely. The Ascendancy's reign is ending."

"What?" I asked, wrinkling my forehead.

His use of the word *reign* was a peculiar choice, in my opinion. A reminder of early history, where countries were headed under the ruling of a monarch. The Ascendancy's form of governing couldn't be further off—no singular person dominated over the other. Rather, the Ascendancy was headed by a group of men, all with different roles in regards to different sectors of the government.

Pater, who I realized had retrieved a small device from somewhere amongst the clutter on the table, turned his back to me. A screen, embedded within the concrete walls behind them, came to life, the light emitting from the screen washing over the contents of the room.

The news broadcast from that evening filled on the screen: the image of streets, once occupied by thousands of families, now filled with remains and rubble.

I tore my eyes away, averting my gaze toward the exit.

Why are they showing me this?

To boast about the lives they'd taken?

To assert their thirst for power and control through the senseless murders of the young and the poor?

Bile burned against the back of my throat.

"This destruction and pain is a product of the Ascendancy," Tata said, rising from his chair and circling around the table to tower over me. "Murus Amissa killed those people."

THIRTEEN

SILENS

Still standing feet away from the edge of the table, refusing to give his fathers the satisfaction of sitting under their upturned noses, Treyton watched as Tata rounded the table to loom over Miles.

The Ascendant woman had turned away from the horrific images displayed on the screen behind him, shrinking down into her chair. Though already petite, she appeared even smaller underneath Tata's broad figure. It was only when Tata mentioned her father's responsibility for the wide-scale attack within the Ascendancy that her head snapped upward to glare at him.

"He did no such thing," she said, her voice breaking.

Even though she was fighting to defend her father, it was clear that even she was struggling to believe his innocence.

Tata leaned down to speak into her ear.

"He ordered officials to detonate the virus that slaughtered those people. The Ascendancy are uncivilized. *Animals*. To them, the death of innocents is a worthy price to pay to reinforce their power. They strike fear into the hearts of their citizens so that those same citizens will turn to them at the first sign of disaster."

Miles sank deeper into her chair. "That's not true," she said, shaking her head.

The muscles in Treyton's legs lurched as he watched her squirming under his father's badgering like a cornered rabbit. But springing to her defense would only have Tata questioning his loyalty, and a frustrated Tata would only be more difficult on the young woman.

The angrier his father got, the harder he would press.

"I can assure you," Tata said, stroking the hair on her head like a parent comforting a crying infant, "everything I say is the truth."

The sight made Treyton bilious. Even for Tata, touching and stroking her trembling head was a step out of line. Treyton had assured her on her own porch steps that she could put her trust in him. But then, under the scrutiny of his father, Treyton could sense her mistrust. It might as well have been written plainly across her face in bold, black lettering.

Miles wrinkled her nose. "Your assurance means nothing to me."

"And why should it? You're just Ascendant scum."

Miles' jaw fell.

"I think you've made your point," Treyton interjected, his words laced with verbal venom. Forcing her into submission through tactics of fear and confusion went against everything the Resiliens' work stood for. Decades of trying to protect the lives of innocents through knowledge and understanding, demeaned by every word Tata was spitting.

If he stood by and allowed his father to act in such a jeopardizing manner, he was no better than those of the Ascendancy.

"If I'd made my point, none of us would be here," Tata shot back, his hand still resting atop Miles' head. She'd brought her knees up to her chest, her head hanging so that the dark tresses that had escaped her ponytail veiled her face.

"She's just one person. You can't push this all on her. She isn't the Ascendancy, and she isn't her father."

Pater lifted himself out of his chair, switching the display off before setting the remote on the table in front of him. "Treyton is right. You're taking things a tad too far."

A tad? Treyton scoffed.

"Too far? This is Murus Amissa's *kid* we're talking to. I don't trust her as far as I can throw her."

"Oh," Pater answered, his eyes lacking their usual warmth. "So now we're allowed to talk about children?"

Tata held Pater's gaze. Treyton silently thanked his ancestors for the table separating the sides of the room, preventing either of them from acting out in a way that they would later come to regret.

"Could you focus on the matter at hand?" Tata growled, slamming his fist on the table.

Miles flinched, burying her face into the crook of her arm.

"Have you lost your mind?" Pater hissed, raising his own voice in order to match Tata's. He was at a disadvantage, however. His voice was softer by nature. When he yelled, it sounded forced. Strained. Like a nightingale singing out from a high point in the sky.

Deciding that he had heard enough of their dispute, Treyton clambered up onto the table to stand in between them. To his amusement, everyone in the room set aside their quarrels and regarded him and his theatrics with wide eyes.

"I would like to kindly ask all of you to pull your undies out of your a—"

"Treyton Silens Venus," Tata growled, cutting Treyton short. "I order you to come down from there this instant!"

"No can do, Daddio."

Adrenaline pumped through his veins, igniting a fire that danced within his chest. Though he was only a few feet off the ground, his heart soared. It was as though he had climbed the highest-standing mountain on Earth and was peering out over the rolling hills.

The rolling hills that he had only seen in paintings and other artistic depictions. His "career path" didn't exactly allow for weekend-long trips into the countryside to hike mountains. If Treyton willed the thought hard enough, he could almost imagine the wind ruffling his hair and kissing the bare skin of his cheeks.

"I won't repeat myself, young man. Down. *Now.*"

"Only if you come up here and get me yourself, old man."

A smirk tugged at Treyton's lips. There was something satisfying about defying not only his superior, but his father.

Tata's slackened jaw and wide eyes were an image worth any threat of punishment he could bestow.

"You're acting inappropriately in front of our guest," Pater said with a frown.

Treyton peered out of the corner of his eyes at Miles, who had dropped her knees from her chest. The corners of her mouth twitched as she tried to fight back a smile. When their eyes met, she lifted her hand to shield her lips. But even so, a light still kindled in her eyes. She found amusement in his shenanigans, and he was glad to diffuse the tension and whirlwind of violent emotion that plagued the room. Even if it meant getting an earful from his parents later, which he would spend the following week living down.

Before he could leap out of the way, something sharp jabbed at his ribcage. His legs buckled underneath him, the shock knocking some of the air from his lungs and sending his heart into a frenzy. He twisted his head to look up. James hovered over him, and his face held no emotion. A blank, inanimate slate. Treyton turned to look to Tata for an explanation or a word in his defence, but the older man only turned up his nose.

That told him everything he needed to know.

James, obedient to a fault, had come to Tata's aid, once more earning his stamp of approval. Not that it was worth anything. Their parents' approval was a symbol of one thing, and one thing only—the sacrifice of one's own free will.

Treyton curled his fingers around the hand grip of his gun, which was still tucked away in its holster. He swung his arm and the weapon in the direction of James' knees, but before the gun could connect, James stomped his foot down, pinning Treyton's arm to the table with ease.

He twisted his arm, trying to tug it out from beneath his brother's weight, but the process only sent a flare of pain tearing through his shoulder.

"Agh!"

Miles thrust her chair back as she barrelled to her feet.

"Stop that!" she shouted. "Seriously, what is *wrong* with you people? Jumping up on tables, throwing each other around like a bunch of wild animals!"

Her entire demeanor had changed. Before, she'd been cowering in her chair. Now her upper lip curled back, and she had a harsh squint about her face, as though having a difficult time decoding the dynamic in front of her.

She'll get used to it, Treyton thought with a self-satisfied grin.

"You brought me here for a reason," she continued. "We had a deal. And now you're just wasting my time." Miles tilted her chin, a newfound swell of confidence seeming to inflate her self-esteem. "If we're done, I'd like to go home."

"Home is no longer an option," James answered, much to Treyton's surprise. Up until that point, his older brother had made a point of engaging with the young woman as little as possible. "We cannot risk you being an obstruction by returning you home to alert your authorities."

"What if I give you my word?" she asked, wrapping her arms around herself.

Her self-esteem was deflating again.

"I won't even tell them who you are," she insisted. "I'll just say that I went out for a walk or something. Just tell me where Quercus is and I'll find my way back myself."

Just as easily as she'd emerged from within her shell, she'd returned to it, fleeing from any threat of confidence.

Treyton ground his teeth. What was so wrong with her that she couldn't stand up for herself for more than forty-five seconds? Besides, she wasn't stupid. She had to know what she was suggesting was poorly thought out, and not at all a reason that his parents—members of the council—would accept. Of everybody he had ever met, she was the only person who teetered between ferocity and sensitivity to the point of tears.

She was at war with herself.

Two minds in one body.

Pater frowned. "Like I said, I know this can't be an easy adjustment for you to make, and I apologize on behalf of my family for their behaviour. But you can't leave."

Circling the table, Pater stopped a few feet short of her, seeming to notice the mounting anxiety in her body language—rapid, short breaths; moon-round eyes; clenched fingers.

"We want to allow you the freedom to make your own decisions, of course," said Pater. "We want you to take what we're saying and believe it to be true but, more importantly, we want you to side with what you believe to be ethically and morally just."

"And if I decide that you're all just a bunch of madmen?" The Ascendant woman lifted her chin, keeping otherwise still.

"If you decide to rebel, or at any time attempt to escape the confines of this base and endanger our people, you will be imprisoned, despite my best intentions," Tata answered for his husband.

The harsh, grinding sound of wood against the old cement floor as Tata guided her chair up behind her made the hairs along Treyton's neck prickle with unease. Gesturing that she take a seat again, his father twisted his mouth into a satisfied grin. In compliance, she sat and tugged the chair forward so that her chest was pressed against the edge of the table.

"Whatever it is you want from me," she said, reaching up to brush a lock of escaped hair from her eyes, "you're wasting your time. Murus is a man of his own accord."

The way she spoke about her father made Treyton twitch. From the lack of emotion behind her words, it seemed that her relationship with her father was held together by a rapidly unravelling thread. Then again, who was he to make assumptions about the nature of someone's relationship with their family?

He cleared his throat, recalling that he was still pinned at the arm underneath James' boot, splayed out across the table they spoke across. When James lifted his foot, he rolled off to the side before landing on his feet. James hopped down beside him.

"It's understandable why you would be reluctant to believe us," Tata, who still lingered behind her, said. "And if we can't convince you of our innocence, perhaps you'd be more interested in hearing from a familiar face."

The young woman moved to kneel in the chair, turning to grip its spine. She narrowed her eyes. "Pardon me?"

"We're not your foe, Miss Amissa. And it seems clear to me that the only way to reach you is through compromise. In exchange for an open mind, we're prepared to reunite you with an…old friend."

Treyton leaned forward, straining his ears to hear what his father was saying with certainty.

What on God's green earth is that *supposed to mean?*

"It's my understanding that you've been acquainted with Major Salices," Tata continued. He strolled toward the exit, hands deep in his pockets. With a curt nod to someone standing on the other side of the small, rectangular pane of glass constructed within the door, the steel slab was nudged open, and into the room slipped one of the

Arxmen that had been standing outside the infirmary.

Straining his eyes, Treyton recognized the scar extending over his chin. It was the same man who'd been careful to keep his face hidden from them, and he suspected it was not because the scar was unsightly.

The Arxman removed his hat, revealing tousled tufts of ruddy hair. Without anything to obstruct Treyton's view of the man's face, a realization emerged.

Quercus Salices, in the flesh.

In the image presented to James, himself, and the other sector heads, he'd been only a young boy with sunken eyes and hollowed cheeks. The man standing before them now had a fuller face and years of experience etched into the corners of his eyes, and his chin was rough with patches of unshaven hair. Even still, the resemblance was impossible to deny.

"What the hell is this?" The words cannoned out of Treyton's mouth, and he jabbed a finger in the man's—Quercus'—direction. "Death sentence, my ass!"

Quercus folded his arms, hat still in hand. "Had I known there would be children in attendance, I would have worn my light-up sneakers."

Treyton grit his teeth against the remark.

"One of the midnight patrols found him wandering the tunnels with no recollection of how he'd escaped or how he'd arrived," Tata responded with a level tone.

"Smells like fish," Treyton muttered under his breath, pinching his nose closed. Quercus only looked him up and down before turning his attention elsewhere.

Following his gaze, it seemed Fish-Boy was observing Miles for her reaction.

Treyton's gut did a somersault.

FOURTEEN

MILES

A breath caught in my throat, making it difficult for me to speak. Thoughts and questions—was he really Quercus? Alive? Not in danger, but safe and standing less than ten feet from me?—formed in my mind, perching themselves on the end of my tongue. But no matter how hard I fought to speak, the words refused.

At first, I could hear the others speaking amongst one another—about where he'd come from; how he'd gotten there. I lifted my knees to my chest, careful not to allow my legs to dangle over the side of the chair in case I'd somehow stumbled my way into a nightmare. A grotesque monster lurked beneath me, ready to clamp onto my leg and tow me down into the earth's hellish core.

I began to draw up ideas in my mind about what the monster might look like. Perhaps he wore a suit, or had eyes the colour of bile.

Maybe we were relatives.

The feeling of probing eyes drew me back to the present. I lifted my head, trying to suppress my emotions from seeping through to my facial expressions. They'd already stolen my thoughts. Taken my words. If I surrendered to them my feelings, I would have nothing left to call my own. And though the thought had crossed my mind on more than one occasion since my arrival, I wasn't sure that I was ready to commit to the idea of erasing myself from existence.

"Miles?"

I swallowed hard. *He* was looking at me. Expecting a reaction out of me. Expecting me to jump up and down or wrap my arms around his neck in a warm embrace.

Clenching my jaw, I blinked back the hot tears that welled in my eyes.

How dare he.

Ten years I'd wondered where he'd disappeared to without so much as a word about where he was going or an invitation to join him.

Before my interaction with the Salices, I'd spent ten years wondering whether or not their son was even alive, or if he'd been euthanized at the hands of the Ascendancy.

If I would ever hear from him again.

Ten years I'd hoped in my heart that my protector, my *friend*, would return. And now that he stood in front of me, wearing a smug smile like a badge of honour, I resented him. He didn't get to waltz back into my life as though he'd never left at all.

"Hi," I said. That was all I could muster without betraying how much I wanted to slap him. To leave a lasting mark on his skin, like the mark he'd left on me—a constant reminder that he wasn't available. But the longer he pointed his gentle eyes in my direction, as familiar to me now as when I was twelve, the more my heart began to soften.

The longer I ached to rest my head against him and breathe in rhythm with the rise and fall of his chest, the larger the fracture in my heart grew. Cursing myself inwardly for being attracted to the idea, I lifted myself out of my chair, but refused to cross the distance

between us should he try to pull me into a hug.

"You remember me, don't you?" he asked. "Unless I'm not as memorable as I thought."

I spit the words: "I do."

He took a step forward, breaching the invisible line I'd drawn between us as he crept closer, his green eyes homing in on me. My own began to search his face for insincerity, or a telling sign that the man standing before me was only wearing Quercus' identity. But behind the scars, like strokes of white paint splashed across his chin and forehead, and the lines forming around his thin lips, he was the spitting image of the boy I'd spent my leisure hours with. Even if he were to curl back his lip, or draw his eyebrows together to scowl, I would know. Quercus' eyes had always had a gentleness to them that made people want to trust him.

Like I had.

"Hey," he said and rested a hand on my shoulder, giving it a squeeze. "You're shaking like a leaf."

I jerked out from under his grasp, cutting my gaze to the wall on the opposite side of the room. I'd been so preoccupied with keeping my face still that I hadn't even realized I was trembling all over.

"I'm fine," I hissed.

"The reunion we've all been waiting for," Silens quipped. He'd finally chosen to seat himself, kicking his legs up onto the table. He clapped, leaning back into his chair. "Now would someone care to explain to me just what in the name of *hell* is going on here? I thought this guy was—oh, what's the word?—dying!"

I relaxed a little. I'd begun to think I was losing my mind and slipping into madness. At least now I knew that I wasn't the only one wanting answers to similar questions.

"Or have we been graced with the presence of a ghost?" The light in Silens' eyes darkened.

"Now that we're all here, there is something we should admit to you all," Pater answered. "Quercus was never in any danger. When reviewing Miss Amissa's archives, including the results from her psychiatric evaluations, we inferred that willing her to comply would be easier in theory than in practice. We understood that approaching a young woman, brought up by a man like Murus, would present its challenges. That her beliefs would be all but set in stone. Persuading her to look through a new lens meant that we needed motivation. Something, or *someone*, personal to her."

A wave of nausea brushed up against my esophagus. Though I was present in the room, they spoke about me as though I were elsewhere. As if I were back at home, still a servant under the Ascendancy's reign. And much to my dismay, to call that place *home* fired a chill down my spine.

"So you manipulated her?" Silens removed his feet from off the table, his legs planted like roots into the ground as he leaned forward, his jaw twitching. The man didn't seem to know how to sit still, vibrating under the intensity of his emotions. "Isn't that what you mean to say?"

"If you wish to put it in such an abhorrent way," Tata answered for his husband.

A cold draft sank its teeth into the back of my neck, sending an aftershock rippling down the length of my spinal column. I'd thought that Silens had lied to me, that he'd only said that Quercus would die without my cooperation in order to get me to open my front door and follow him there. But now, seeing how he picked his father's mind for a clearer understanding, it seemed to me that he was just as out of the loop as I was.

Quercus folded his arms. "Like you had any better ideas, beefcake."

My eyes searched the redhead's face now that his attention was turned toward Silens. Underneath the broiling hostility written into his expression was a thin layer of ease. Comfort, maybe. As though this interaction were the definition of normalcy.

Had Quercus known about the Resiliens all along?

I racked the memory of my youth—of him—for signs that might have hinted toward this new theory of mine. If he had, he'd been careful not to leave a trail. And even if he hadn't, how could he betray his own father now? And how could he betray Murus, his mentor?

I could understand him betraying me. I was only the neighbourhood's token girl, after all. Betrayal had become my friendly acquaintance.

"Settle down, both of you," Pater ordered, returning to his seat with a tired sigh. "Miss Amissa, please feel free to ask questions. Express your concerns. Anything that might make this transition easier for you."

"What transition?" I asked.

Lowering myself back into my seat, I folded my hands together in my lap. My mind was whirling, trying to piece together everything I'd heard so far. But every bit of understanding seemed to wriggle away, too far out of my reach for me to grasp. I couldn't tell if I should try to befriend these people or curse them for committing treason.

After all, they hadn't made any effort to prove what they were claiming was true. They had no evidence to prove that my father was a murderer, nor that they weren't the guilty party responsible for the deaths of thousands of Ascendant citizens.

"The Ascendancy is corrupt," Pater began. "They punish the innocent and discard the poor, all to reap the benefit of control. Their governing was meant to be a good thing for humankind, to preserve peace and maintain equity. But when voted into power, it only took a matter of months for them to take back what they'd promised.

"So, to answer your question, we want to transition you into the Resiliens. To understand and speak on behalf of the truth."

"All I hear are words," I retorted.

With a curt nod of his head, Pater once again retrieved the rectangular device from off the table. A moment later, a new broadcast—of a man sitting in his office—was displayed on the screen.

As I leaned forward, taking in the image, I recognized the towering bookshelves and the large oak desk that took up a majority of the remaining space in the room.

Murus' office.

The man sitting at the desk was Murus, hammering away at his keyboard, exchanging correspondence with one of his many business associates, I expected.

"What is this?" I asked, looking to Pater for an explanation. The older man only put a finger to his lips, asking for my silence.

"Good evening, sir."

Another man with brownish-blond hair had entered my father's office and seated himself in the empty chair opposite him. His face was rough with facial hair.

"I'm here in regards to your demands. You're certain?"

Murus' fingers fell still against the keyboard. "Are you questioning my authority?"

"Not at all, sir. But there are roughly eighty-four thousand people living within those compounds. If we go through with this, there is no mitigating the ramifications."

Murus rose from his chair, bracing himself against his desk. His eyebrow twitched. "You will do as you're told or you'll be joining them."

"Very well, sir."

The broadcast ended, and the screen faded to black.

A scream bubbled in my chest. My throat was raw, and my cheeks were damp with tears. Murus was a terrible man, I'd known that much. He'd always been ornery and narcissistic, doing nothing if not for his own personal gain. But I'd never thought him a mass murderer.

I shook my head, trying to clear the fog engulfing my thoughts. There had to be *some* explanation. But no matter how I tried to construct the details, all of the evidence pointed back to the same conclusion.

The reasoning for his actions didn't matter—whatever it was, it wasn't worth destroying thousands of lives.

I thought of the broadcast from that morning.

The lifeless bodies lining the sidewalks and the haunting stares of blank eyes.

Eyes that would never see again.

Lives that were taken too soon.

My stomach contracted. I leapt out of my chair and hunched over the ground. With violent convulsions, the contents of my stomach forced their way into the back of my throat before being expelled in a pool in front of me.

A hand rubbed my back in slow, circular motions. I sat back on my rear, combing away the loose strands of hair that clung to my mouth. The smell of vomit made a home in my nostrils, threatening to induce another bout.

When my body finally began to ease and I was no longer afraid of the possibility of vomiting a second time, I looked to see who knelt next to me.

Quercus.

"Get away from me," I breathed, my voice hoarse due to the burning sensation in my throat.

"I'm here," he whispered and wrapped his arms around my shoulders.

Weight built up in my chest, threatening to explode. "Please," I begged. "Get off of me."

But Quercus didn't let go. He buried his face into the top of my head, his words muffled by my hair as he murmured, "You're safe

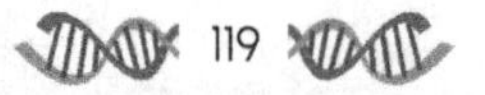

now."

I couldn't understand his eagerness to hold me and to assure me that everything would be all right. Everything *wasn't* all right. I wasn't safe. There wasn't one aspect to the entire scenario that even remotely suggested that everything was as it should be. I tried to pull away from him again, but he only squeezed his arms tighter.

"Let me go!" I screamed.

Quercus' arms slipped from around my shoulders, and the weight in my chest alleviated. I glanced up to ensure that he'd moved a satisfying distance away, only to find myself staring at the back of Silens' leg. Rising to my feet and peering around him, I could see that Quercus knelt on the ground in front of him, the pinkish beginnings of a red mark flourishing on one side of his face.

"You scum," Silens said through clenched teeth. Though the words were directed at Quercus, they were so full of contempt that a shudder swayed my body.

Spitting bloodied saliva on the ground, Quercus wiped at his mouth with the back of his hand. "I'll kill you."

The ferocity with which he spoke made my stomach clench again.

Silens folded his arms across his chest. "I'd like to see you try," he challenged.

The two men held each other's gazes, their hostility unwavering. Worried that one might pounce and start clawing at the other's eyes with their fingernails, I tugged at Silens' hand, trying to divert his attention.

"It's okay…"

Before I could catch him, Silens dropped to the ground like a dead weight. I brought my hands up to my face, covering my gaping mouth as I watched him writhe on the floor.

His limbs flopped this way and that; his eyes rolled into the back of his head. Like some sort of seizure.

"Silens," I called, unable to hear the surrounding voices in the room above my own panic.

No response.

Silens' body was still flailing—the longer he seized, the more aggressive the convulsions became.

"Silens," I called again, louder this time, throwing myself onto my hands and knees next to him. I took his shoulders in my hands, trying to keep him still despite his violent jerking. The tightening in my torso constricted my lungs.

"What's wrong with him?" I cried, trying to fight the tremble from my voice.

"Currens, go fetch Miss Davis," Tata ordered his son, who was already sprinting for the exit, his authoritative voice slicing through the roar of terror rumbling around me. As Currens disappeared through the steel doors, someone seized my arms from behind.

"What the—?"

One of the men lined up against the wall—what they called an Arxman—was twisting my arms behind my back, pressing my wrists between my shoulder blades. A fiery pinching in my spine made me squirm, but their grip on me was firm. The Arxman forced me to the wall, my cheek cold against the cement. If it weren't for the shock, or perhaps my persistent confusion, I might have sooner noticed the sharp pain from the guard's hold lighting a fire in my shoulders as he leaned his weight into my body.

"No," I said, shaking my head. I planted my feet, trying to stand my ground.

To fight back.

"Let me go!"

A vein was beginning to form on the man's forehead. He lifted one of his hands to grip a clump of my hair, forcing my face harder against the wall, the cement scraping the surface of my cheek and burning my face.

"On your knees," he grunted.

With a defiant growl, I thrust my head back, connecting with the guard's forehead and stunning him long enough to break away from his grasp. But before I'd made it more than three feet away, his arm snaked around my waist, cradling my body to his.

Disadvantageous in weight, my feet slipped out from underneath me and I stumbled, the wall creeping closer once again.

"I didn't do anything wrong!"

And that much was true. I'd only tried to call Silens' attention away before the two men had tried to kill one another. How could I have known he would just collapse and start to seize?

This isn't my fault!

"Agh!" The sound erupted from my lungs as I fought to tear my arms from the man's grasp, hurtling myself backward, away from the wall and into his chest. This secondary act of defiance, unanticipated by the Arxman, caught him off guard. His grasp on me faltered enough that I was able to jerk out of his hold again. I made it three paces to the exit, thinking that I might be able to outrace them if I could only make it out to the tunnels, before the blur of another man hurled into me and tackled me to the ground.

Defeated. Again.

The collision made my skeleton groan, and there was a flaring pain in my lungs as I gulped mouthfuls of air, this type of activity more than my untrained body was capable of. I was no Ascendant officer or trained assassin. I was only a girl. Weak. Fragile. Meant to feel pain and endure it, if only to survive.

Under the man's weight, I battered at him with my fists. Clenching his jaw, he forced me over onto my chest, bringing my arms behind my back.

Before I could try to fight my way out from underneath him in another attempt at escape, my wrists were bound. Not by rope or metal, but by some sort of fabric that he wrapped around my wrists.

The fabric was soft against my skin, yet no matter how hard I fought to tear my hands free, the fabric wouldn't give.

What the…?

"Seriously?" I said incredulously. What kind of a twisted joke were they playing at?

"Seriously."

The familiar voice made my skin crawl.

Quercus.

"Let me go, or I swear—"

"What?" A grin twisted his lips as I peered over my shoulder at him. "Know when to give up, love."

A lump formed in my throat. Only one word was compatible with the movement of my lips.

"Why?"

"Because you're outnumbered, and you're overpowered. Fighting me will only make this worse for you."

"But why are *you* doing this? I didn't do anything! You were supposed to be my friend."

I pretended not to hear the crack in my voice.

Quercus' eyes dimmed. "I am your friend. And as your friend, I'm telling you this because you need to hear it: Stop fighting it."

Stop fighting *what*?

I grit my teeth and tore my eyes away.

He wasn't my friend. Any friend of mine wouldn't have me pinned to the cold cement floor against my will—and for no reason!

The man holding me looked and sounded identical to Quercus, though an older version of himself, but I couldn't believe that he was who he claimed to be.

I wouldn't.

If I did, it meant that everything I'd thought I'd known about him was a lie. And Quercus was the only person I needed to be certain about. Or so I'd thought.

I let my muscles relax. Regardless of his identity or our history together, what he was telling me held still *some* truth. I *was* outnumbered, and he was far too heavy to fight off. If I meant to stay alive, I would have to cooperate. Whatever that meant.

Quercus hoisted me to my feet and guided me away from the commotion. From the corner of my eye, I could see Silens still convulsing. During my attempt at escape, Currens must have returned with Klara, because the two of them now hovered over his brother, Pater and Tata lingering a few feet from the others with their arms entangled in a form of embrace.

I spotted a syringe in Klara's hand. Currens was trying to hold Silens still while Klara moved the needle to inject some substance—an anticonvulsant, I guessed, from the little I'd read about seizures in the archives—into Silens' arm. But before the needle could pierce his skin, I was guided out of the room by Quercus. Another Arxman brought up the rear of our group.

As we passed through the steel doors, a chilling thought fought its way to the foreground of my mind. What if I *was* at fault for Silens' seizure? Before I'd touched his hand, he'd been fine, fired up, with a glow to his skin and a gleam in his eyes fueled by the clear hostility between him and Quercus. To see him writhing on the ground, his face burning red and beads of sweat forming on his forehead, arms and legs thrashing—my stomach did another somersault and I thought I might be sick again.

Let him be okay, I thought.

I fought against the fabric binding my wrists together one last time as though, by some miracle, the fabric might just give way.

That I'd be free.

That I'd be shaken awake and released from the twisted, prolonged nightmare that I'd been walking for twenty-two years.

But the fabric held up. And any hope that I'd had that this reality was not my own fell away yet again.

I'm so screwed.

FIFTEEN

MILES

Like most children, I'd been warned by my dad never to play with fire. It had seemed like common sense. After all, who would willingly hold their hand over a flame and watch as their skin first sweltered and then blackened?

Having taken my dad's warning to heart, I'd never been burnt, nor experienced the crippling pain that I imagined came with torching the thousands of nerve endings in one's hand.

The room was illuminated by candlelight.

Orange.

Flickering.

As I watched the flame twirl, an idea struck me. If I could make it over to the fire, I could try and burn the fabric binding my wrists, freeing myself. But without the use of my hands, I'd have to rise to my feet from the ground and practice caution in doing so, using only my knees as leverage.

I rocked forward, the cement rough against the bottoms of my legs even with the material of my pants acting as a semi-protective barrier.

"Careful, Miles," I warned myself aloud. Though I supposed there was no real risk in losing my balance and falling forward, falling face-first might result in a not-so-pleasant scrape or, at the very least, a sore nose.

Lifting one of my legs and placing my foot flat against the ground, I managed to stand up.

From my earlier place on the ground, the room had appeared much smaller—an illusion brought on by the black paint coating the surrounding walls. But now, standing up, I could see that the space was much larger than my own quarters back at Murus' base. The lack of furnishings only made it all the more unwelcoming.

Lonesome, even.

Inching closer toward the candle, I realized the flaw in my plan. Granted, said plan had come to me in the spur of the moment—a plan resting on a foundation of desperation.

The candle was anchored to the wall above my head. Unless I could dislocate both of my shoulders, there was no way I could reach up high enough to hold the fabric to the flame. With a sigh, I fell back against the wall, careful not to hit my head on the candle holder.

Now what?

Something caught my attention from the corner of my eye. Markings on the wall. They were disorderly and appeared as though their maker had once known English but had lost their knowledge of the dialect after years of containment and separation.

I imagined these markings might have been their last attempt at leaving their mark on the world.

I'd never had—or been allowed—much of an imagination growing up. An active imagination, according to Murus, meant that one was simply distracted. It was a sign of unreliability.

Tracing the grey markings, I tried to imagine who their maker might have been; how they'd found themselves trapped in this very room; what they might have looked like.

If they'd died on this very floor, their hands bound by the same resistant fabric…

I pictured a shorter girl, like myself, but with blonde hair. Large blue eyes, maybe. The more difference I placed on this imaginary girl, who more likely than not never existed at all, the more I assured myself that my fate would be different.

They can't keep me in here forever.

But I was lying to myself. Of course they could keep me there—I doubted that a group rebelling against the sole form of government was at all law-abiding. I was only trying to keep a positive outlook in order to preserve what remained of my sanity. It was uncertain how long I would be trapped in that room. How long it would be until I saw the sun or was given access to water, if at all. Having a psychotic break less than two hours into being a…

A hostage?

The term felt prickly as I let it roll off my mind's tongue.

Captive was more the term that I was looking for. After all, there was no wager to be made with my life. No one would come to save me.

I scanned the room with my eyes, searching for the entrance. After Quercus and the other Arxman had left, the door's edges had faded away, cloaked using technology that I knew nothing about.

Vibrations rocked the ground beneath my feet, jostling my nerves to life. On the opposite end of the room, blue light filtered in as the door's edges appeared and the door cracked open. A carnivorous kaleidoscope of butterflies gnawed at the insides of my stomach.

The same woman that had met us—myself, Silens, Currens, and Rupedo—in the tunnels stepped into the room, both of her hands sheltered by the pockets of her long overcoat.

Like Silens' and Currens', her coat was also embellished by gold-and-white needlework. Her coat, however, had additional red beading sewn into the collar.

As she marched across the room toward me, the mingled fragrance of vanilla and sea salt swept over me. The scent might have been soothing if it weren't so overpowered by the acidity in the older woman's narrowed eyes.

"You've caused quite a stir, Miss Amissa," she said, her words slow.

"Is Silens okay?"

I held still against the wall, tugging at the end of my coat's sleeve. My coat, made of white linen, was in stark contrast to what I'd seen of their aesthetics in apparel, making me stand out a mile further than I already did.

To my surprise, the woman offered me a small, sympathetic smile.

"He's currently resting in the medical wing," she said. "Miss Davis has assured me that there will be no lasting physical effects, but that amount of trauma on one's body is exhausting."

With a heavy sigh, I slumped against the wall. I slid down until my bottom landed against the cement floor, bringing my knees up to cradle them in my arms.

"I don't know what happened," I insisted.

"*You* happened."

Was that an accusation? My pulse jittered.

"But I didn't do anything. He just—"

"But you did," the woman interrupted, inching closer. "You felt threatened, so you defended yourself."

My eyes sharpened into a challenging glare. We'd known each other for less than thirty seconds and she—a stranger—was already making assumptions about my character.

"What are you on about?"

Cocking an eyebrow, the woman folded her arms. "Since you seem so certain about what didn't happen, why don't you go ahead and tell me what did?"

I kicked into overdrive, scouring my mind for an explanation. For proof of my innocence. But I fell short, left with only the cloudy memory of fluttering limbs and the whites of Silens' eyes.

"It wasn't my fault." The words fell out of my mouth before I'd taken the time to think them over.

The bones in my body jittered next. And, judging by the brief flash of annoyance that passed over the woman's critical stare, I was beginning to realize that I was only digging myself a deeper, roomier grave.

"Well, you're not entirely wrong about that," she answered, her voice hushed to a whisper.

My ears twitched at that.

The lines carving out the woman's mouth softened, as did her eyes. "Our plans relied on you already knowing of your ability."

Ice lined my veins. "My what?"

"The inhuman begin displaying their abilities around the age of eighteen. But it would appear that you've developed later than usual. Likely a result of unconscious repression."

I wrapped my arms tighter around myself. The woman spoke as though she were reciting a paragraph out of an archive.

"But I'm not an inhuman."

I was beginning to think that these people were delusional, telling themselves stories and believing them to be true in order to manipulate me into accepting their narrative.

The woman gathered her hair in her hands before pulling it forward so that it sloped over her chest in long umber waves.

"Whether or not you choose to believe me is your decision to make, but the fact of the matter still remains. You *are* inhuman."

"That...That's impossible," I said, stumbling over my own words.

An inhuman? I combed through my memories, trying to recall a moment in time where the possibility might have struck me.

Then I scolded myself for even searching for such a possibility.

Of course I wasn't an inhuman. Like all citizens of the Ascendancy, born on and after the day of the *Regeneratio*, my genetic material had been manipulated as an embryo to ensure that such an incident would not occur.

The woman drew close enough now that if I had reached out my hand, I could have traced the fine lines under her eyes with a finger. The name tape sewn into her uniform over the right side of her chest, peeking out from beneath locks of her hair, revealed her name: *L.G. Alessandra Martins.*

Alessandra put her hand against my cheek—a small gesture that might have been ordinary between two old friends but was not between two strangers. My muscles tightened under her touch as I tried to hold myself still, unsettled by the woman's eagerness to feel a stranger's face in such an intimate manner.

"Let me prove it to you."

"Prove what?"

I expected to see the woman's eyes harden with frustration, but found caressing pools of sympathy in their place. Pools that I found myself wanting to wade into until I could find the courage to take the plunge.

Alessandra's hand fell away from my face. "Turn around."

I hesitated, worried that I'd said something to offend her, before turning my back to her as instructed.

Alessandra's fingers brushed against my wrists before the fabric tying them together slackened and I was able to free my hands. The fabric drifted to rest at my feet, and I lifted my hands to inspect them.

There wasn't a single red mark. No visible indication that suggested I'd been bound at all.

"Why did you untie me?" I asked, turning back around to face her.

"Because trust is a two-way street," she answered, bending down to retrieve the fabric from off the ground. "The sooner you learn to

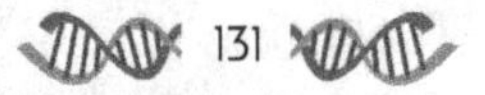

trust us, the sooner we'll learn to trust you."

"You're saying I should just take your word for it?"

"No." The word was sharp as it shot from her mouth, like an iron ball fired from a cannon. "Never take anyone's word for anything. Ask questions, look for answers. But sometimes"—Alessandra flashed me a broad smile—"don't be so afraid to trust people."

"And that includes you?"

Alessandra gave a short laugh, juggling the strip of black fabric between her hands. The sound of her laughter was airy, freeing.

Addictive, even.

"Don't make me tie your hands back together."

My lips twitched as I tried to think up a witty response, eager to hear Alessandra's laugh again, but my mind came up short. The heat of embarrassment crept up along the side of my neck. But, determined not to let Alessandra notice the pink glow rising to my cheeks, I turned my face away and decided to revert the topic of the conversation to our earlier subject.

"Still doesn't prove that I'm an inhuman."

"Impatient, aren't we?" Alessandra shifted her weight to one leg, placing a hand on her hip.

I tightened my jaw. What was *that* supposed to mean? I hardly thought myself to be impatient. Given the situation, I'd thought that I'd composed myself quite well. Time was crawling along, and yet I still lacked sufficient answers to the questions I'd come here in light of. These people were tiptoeing around me, careful to dodge any area of conversation that might reveal too much.

If anything, I'd been more than patient.

"Would you relax?" Alessandra nudged me with an elbow. "I'm getting there."

I watched as she strode across the dark room, placing a hand against the wall. The exit cracked open.

"My hero," I mused.

"C'mon," Alessandra said, waving me over. "Unless you'd rather stay here and stare into the void?"

I bounced after her, drinking a breath as we slipped out into the tunnel outside, away from the dark, stifling room. Men and women dressed in black uniforms passed by us in either direction, paying us no mind. Their movements were systematic. Fluent. Almost robotic.

Alessandra leaned toward me. With her face so close to my own, I could count the freckles speckling her brown cheeks.

"The tunnels get kind of crowded during peak hour," she explained. "But you'll fall into the rhythm of things."

I gave a small nod, keeping an eye on those who brushed past. Their faces were fixated on the stretch of tunnel in front of them.

"Lead the way," she said.

A feebleminded proposition, given that I had no clue which direction would lead where. A uniformed man who'd been making his way toward us, following on the heels of two other uniformed men, glared my way, sidestepping out of the way in order to avoid bumping into me. I flinched under his fixated stare.

"God, you startle easy," Alessandra muttered.

"I do not." My eyes trailed after the man as the image of him and his companions grew smaller with distance.

Without responding, Alessandra turned to start in the direction opposite of where the uniformed men had gone. I followed after her, my thoughts racing as Alessandra's claim clung to the forefront of my mind.

Sure, I flinched under the influence of sudden movements, and words seemed to be especially directed at me when tensions ran high, even when not addressing me. But in general, I thought myself to be calm. A voice of reason in times of stress. As the vice-chancellor's daughter, I'd been trained to keep a clear head, even when—

An arm snaked around my waist, drawing me toward my attacker. Their other arm came up around my head to cover my eyes before I could react.

Before I could so much as scream for help, he curled an arm around my head, slapping his hand over my mouth to silence me. His other arm snaked around my waist, pulling me closer to him as he leaned his mouth down to my ear.

My stomach fell through to my feet. I thrashed, squirming out of the person's grasp only when their arms gave away. I threw myself back, flattening myself against the tunnel wall, my chest rising and falling in time with my hammering heart.

"My point exactly." Alessandra folded her arms, a satisfied smirk plastered to her face.

I gawked at her. I'd thought Alessandra to be paces in front of me. Yet, somehow, she'd come up behind me instead. The relief alone was enough to ease the bristling panic in my skin.

"Close your jaw before you catch a fly." She brought her hand up to my chin, and my mouth snapped shut.

As we continued down the length of the tunnel, I tried to fend off the visual memory of Alessandra's arm pressed to my waist.

Her freckled cheeks.

Her enticing grin had burned its way into the backs of my eyes.

What is wrong with me?

My thoughts were not my own. They were being fabricated. Tainted by the glamour of Alessandra's intimidating charm.

We came to a stop outside a pair of large steel doors.

"Klara's medical wing," Alessandra said.

I must have worn a quizzical expression, because Alessandra began to explain. "Klara is the head medical examiner, but she's also a keeper of the Resiliens' archives."

Now she was speaking my language.

"Archives?"

Alessandra nodded. "Almost all of our information and records are stored digitally, but we also keep physical copies of this information. Klara is sort of a traditionalist in that sense, but should something happen to our digital files—hacking, that sort of thing—we'll be prepared, thanks to her brilliant little mind."

Things were done much differently by the Ascendancy. Though there were archives still in existence within the Ascendancy, they were outdated by more than four hundred years. Everything now was done digitally, backed up on hundreds of servers that only the most elite members of the Ascendant government had access to.

I recalled the box of archives that I'd borrowed from the curator's base, which was currently tucked safely underneath my bed.

A heaviness gripped at my chest. Had I known that yesterday would be the last time I would flip through those archives and the information they contained, I would have tried harder to retain the numbers. The graphs, statistics. The images. The facts that had long since gone unnoticed by even the trained human eye, overcome by the elements of time and change.

"Behind these doors is all the evidence you'll ever need," Alessandra said, her voice driving a wedge between me and the ache of my thoughts. "But it wouldn't be fair of me to let you walk in there without drilling something into you first."

Drilling? My brows jumped. "Excuse me?"

"Wisdom," Alessandra burst out. "I'm going to drill some *wisdom* into you."

I waited, mentally silencing the swarm of nervous thoughts that buzzed around in my head. Though Alessandra wasn't all that intimidating when she was smiling and carrying a friendly demeanor, her eyes hardened whenever she spoke from a place of seriousness. Any remnant of warmth had drained from her face, leaving only a tall, stern woman in Alessandra's place.

"I know that nothing makes sense right now," she said. "I can't pretend to understand what you're going through or how you're trying to cope with all of this. But I need you to understand that you're not a prisoner here."

Though the words were knotted together with compassion, I could sense the impending lecture. These words, even if they were genuine, were just a cushion meant to soften the incoming blow.

"But if you continue to act like a victim and take comfort in ignorance, the others are going to continue to look at you like a runaway felon rather than an ally.

"Everyone is on edge right now, not just you. We're in the midst of a war we weren't and aren't prepared to win, and we don't know if we ever will be. Everybody here just wants to live a life without fear, but none of us can do that if we're all trying to pretend that the world is fine just the way it is."

When I opened my mouth to interrupt, Alessandra looked daggers at me. I snapped my mouth shut.

"I knew the moment I saw you that you weren't a monster. There isn't an intimidating bone in your body. But the others aren't necessarily going to see you in that same light. There are children worried about the safety of their homes. Mothers and fathers who don't know if they'll be able to trust you because they're too busy looking out for their families. There are real lives being lived within these tunnels. So before you go and get worked up about what does and doesn't make sense, or what is and isn't impossible, remember that we're all just people, too. Regardless of all the crap that your precious, all-knowing Ascendancy propagates."

After Alessandra had finished speaking, the only sound to be heard in the tunnels was the hushed whisper of nearby people. The same people that Alessandra was describing—*rooting for*.

A knot tightened in my stomach. They were all just as afraid of me as I was of them. The only difference between me and them was that they knew where they stood, where their loyalties lay. If I were any more of my father's daughter, I would have already found a way to report my findings, though accidental, back to the Ascendancy.

But that thought hadn't occurred until now. Another reminder to me that I was my own person—not a product of the Ascendancy, or my father, or Mortem, or my dad's death.

As much as I'd failed to acknowledge their—Silens', Klara's, Currens', and Alessandra's—parts in this particular situation, I'd also failed to recognize my own.

I'd been blindsided in all of this. And expecting me to change my every belief and to ignore the history of my people—the history of the Amissa name—by blackmailing me and threatening the well-being of someone, a friend or otherwise, was unfair.

"I'm sorry," I responded finally. Though I was only half invested in the apology, I meant it enough that a weight lifted from my chest. "I'll try to be less"—I gestured to all of me—"this."

"I'm not asking you to be less like yourself. All I ask is that you be less like them."

Without her having to provide confirmation, I already knew who *they* were.

The image of lifeless bodies scattering the sidewalks like leaves in autumn resurfaced, curdling the contents of my stomach.

If what the Venuses were telling me were true—if the Ascendancy was responsible for the deaths of those people—I was working to defend murderers.

If they were lying to me, blackmailing me like they'd done earlier that night, and I gave in and decided to join them, I would be abandoning the very civilization that Murus had helped to build from the ground up in hopes of a better future.

My doubts slinked deeper into the darker parts of my mind, and my fingers trembled.

The door to the medical wing cracked open, and out poked Klara's head.

"I thought I heard voices. You two all right?" The medical practitioner regarded us with round eyes, which then settled on my face. "You look pale."

Before I could object, Klara was taking me by the hand and guiding me to an exam bench inside. The sterile white walls loomed around me, posters of internal systems and organs staring back at my every turn, similar to the images coloring the pages of numerous archives that I'd once skimmed through. Crossing my legs and folding my hands in my lap, I waited until Klara had returned from the back room—which she had disappeared into momentarily—with a file. She flipped through its contents with enough rigour to burn through the pages, if that were possible.

"Well," she said, seemingly to herself. "That's a tad peculiar."

"What is?" I asked, leaning forward as I tried to peer over the edge of the file folder and at the pages contained within.

"Your genetic makeup is—*hm,* how do I put this—strange, compared to the usual genetic makeup I encounter in Ascendant citizens."

Having forgotten that Alessandra, who sat cross-legged on a chair against the wall next to the bed, had followed the two of us inside, my cheeks were set aflame at the sound of her voice.

"Don't tell me she's going to sprout a tail?" she said.

SIXTEEN

MILES

"A TAIL? GOODNESS, NO."

Klara closed the file, setting it down on the bench beside me. "It might be easier to explain if I just show you both. Statistics show that visual aids improve cognition by—"

Alessandra groaned, and Klara's face fell.

"My bad," she said, rubbing at the side of her neck and forcing a tight-lipped smile.

"What do you mean by 'strange'?" I asked, restoring the focus of the conversation.

The question seemed to spark newfound confidence in the young woman. She leaned over me, moving a monitor anchored to the wall by a metallic arm into view. She punched a sequence of numbers onto a virtual keypad, and the display lit up with an array of images.

I furrowed my brow, trying to make sense of the charts and images. I recognized some of their components. One image in particular was similar to that of a genetic screening: a clear layout of someone's genotype.

But there was something unusual about the genotype. Leaning

in closer to the screen, I could see, woven into the genetic coding, an allele that I'd never seen in any of my previous educational studies. And then, as though reading my mind, the monitor highlighted the anomaly with a vibrant neon-green border.

"What is that?" I asked, turning my head to look back at Klara. The woman was beaming back at me, her eyes shifting with thought.

"If only I knew," she answered, gazing wistfully at the monitor. "It's unlike anything I've ever seen. And I've seen *everything*."

Alessandra must have noticed me arching an eyebrow as she leapt up from her spot, for she explained, "Klara has the ability to remember everything that she's ever heard, read, or touched. She's basically an all-knowing encyclopedia."

I nodded my head. I'd have to keep that in mind. I hadn't yet made a fair assessment of the strangers. For all I knew, I was playing into their good-guy facades. If I were to slip up and share so much as a fragment of information that could be used in the undoing of the Ascendancy and, as a result, Murus, I couldn't begin to imagine the repercussions I would face.

As much as I wanted Murus to fall where he stood, he was a cunning and brilliant man. If ever you were to believe you had the upper hand on him, it was only because he wanted you to believe you'd had a chance at all. And if I began to fall too quickly into believing the good intentions of these people that I'd only just met, Murus would come crawling out of the ashes.

"Does she always stare off into space like that?"

I blinked myself back into awareness. Bumps had formed along my arms. Cold sweat clung to the back of my neck, pasting handfuls of damp hair to my skin.

"Apparently," Alessandra answered.

Klara nodded, gesturing with her hand to the highlighted allele. "*This* is the inhumanus gene, s—"

"You're misinformed," I interrupted, the words spilling out of me. "I've seen imaging of the inhumanus gene. It looks nothing like what you have here."

Bad move. Insult was scrawled all over Klara's round face.

"Just like the rest of you citizens, your approach to scientific research is naive," she said.

"Pardon me?"

"The Ascendancy's research of the gene only extended onward for five years after its discovery. Once they realized that they had all the 'proof' they needed to segregate those they could no longer control, curiosity was written out."

Biting my tongue, I wrung my hands in my lap. Even if I were right about the pictured allele being an entirely different gene, I had no place among them; no credibility. They were an established pack, and I was an outsider. A nobody. And no one took kindly to outsiders who overstepped. That should have been obvious, given my twenty-two years of experience under Murus.

A hand rested on top of my own. When my eyes met Alessandra's, the beautiful woman gave me a reassuring nod.

Klara's gaze settled on my lap, and the line that had formed between her eyes softened.

"To put it as simply as I can, you *are* inhuman. There is no doubt about it. But what you see on the screen here does justifiably raise a couple of rather concerning questions."

"Like?" Alessandra pressed for more information. Her attention was captivated now, her hands slipping out of my reach. Regardless, I was grateful for the woman's initiative.

"We know that the Ascendancy ensures that no zygote in even one percentile with the inhumanus gene survives long enough to be transferred as a viable embryo to the gestational carrier. So it's kinda suspicious that one could have slipped through and gone unnoticed for this long, especially with the procedures they have in place meant to test for stuff like this on an annual basis."

I bit my lip, trying to ignore the bile that had made its way up into my esophagus.

An inhuman?

Retracing the images on the screen, I was reminded that the images on the display were of my own genotype, rather than images pulled at random from a database and used for the purpose of education. But I'd had the inhumanus gene ingrained in my memory and *that*, whatever it was, was not it.

Of course I wasn't an inhuman. They had their facts all mixed up. They hadn't a clue what they were talking about.

"You're still not making any sense," I spoke up again, more confident this time. "Whatever it is you think you're reading, it's incorrect. You said yourself that you have no idea what it is, so why go so far as to make such an absurd accusation? An *illegal* accusation!"

Klara ran a hand through her long, dark-brown hair and let out a drawn-out sigh. Her eyes were dim with what I recognized to be emotional exhaustion. Guilt gripped at my gut. I was beginning to sound just like Murus, I realized, and dread sat on my lungs, making it difficult for me to breathe.

It started with emotional manipulation.

And then it ended in the murder of one's spouse.

"You're right about one thing. This isn't your typical inhumanus gene, but that's because it's a genetic variation. So not only is your genotype unusual for an Ascendant citizen, but it's even *more* unusual for an inhuman."

Klara reached over my shoulder again, turning off the display, before occupying the space next to me on the bed.

My stomach churned. The *Unknown*—human's greatest enemy. *He* peered over Klara's shoulder, whispering inaudibly into my ear. As desperate as I was to hear what it was he was saying, no matter how hard I strained to make out his words, all I heard was a gentle hum.

"I've scoured every archive on the planet, both Ascendant and not. Whatever this variation means, it's unknown to both inhuman and human alike. So to answer your question, I have no proof, and there's nothing I can possibly say to make you believe me. But there is one thing I know for certain.

"When I first came into my abilities, I was forced into loneliness by my own senses. Everything I thought I'd understood no longer made sense, and I had to deal with that all on my own."

Loneliness. A chilling, gripping sensation that hollows out the core of your humanity. Tiptoeing on thin ice around your own neighbours, always under the scrutiny of your peers.

All because I was female. The bottom of the food chain. Like a chick amongst a family of coyotes.

"Whether you choose to believe me or not, you're not alone, Miles. If we were anything like the Ascendancy, you'd be a threat. Locked in a cell, or killed on sight. But we aren't the Ascendancy. We've spent our entire lives trying to be anything but. To protect the inhuman, and to provide them with the support they need in order to find comfort within themselves."

Not once could I recall a time where I'd been comfortable. Even when my dad was still alive, he was enamoured by Murus. Murus' word, as much love as my dad had for me, was law. And so, even when I'd spent time with my dad—the only man I'd ever stood to love in a world where I was constantly in the presence of men—I'd had to keep my guard up to some extent.

It wasn't until Klara reached up, wiping the tears from my cheek, that I realized I was crying. My body shuddered with every sob, out of my control as though my mind had detached itself from its capsule. No matter how many times I told my body to stop, the tears continued to roll across my cheeks, falling from the end of my chin and wetting the backs of my hands.

Klara wrapped an arm around me, using her other hand to cradle my head against her chest. The three of us sat in silence. Whether an hour or five minutes passed, I couldn't be sure.

When I was able to pull myself together again, I wiped the remaining tears from my cheeks and gripped the bedsheets, avoiding eye contact with either of them. Crying in front of other people was a sign of vulnerability. A show of weakness. As much as I wanted to be comfortable around them—around anybody, for the first time in my life—I couldn't. Not yet.

Removing her arm from around my shoulder, Klara straightened her back. "I have more to show you, if you're ready." She stared at the wall across from us when she spoke rather than at me, which I was grateful for.

I nodded, giving Klara the go-ahead.

"While I was doing my research and digging through the Ascendancy's digital archives, I did find some test results dating back to your youth. They contain some information that I think you should know."

I nodded again, taking a breath to try and relax myself, lowering my shoulders so that they were no longer hiked up to my ears.

"So far, nobody has been able to master the science of identifying the specific ability that inhumans develop, nor understand how abilities form. But the Pertento method allows us to determine the tier of one's ability even before it becomes active. I'll save you the speech on the history of the Pertento method, but, based on the test results, you're up on the fifth tier."

Numbness spread throughout my body.

I'd come across the Pertento method in my earlier studies, so that wasn't the part that I found shocking. It was the fact that I, someone who had gone my entire life knowing that I was human, was now no longer human.

That I'd never *been* human.

I was an inhuman, and not just any inhuman, but an inhuman

with a fifth-tier ability. Up until then, a fifth-tier ability had only been a theory—Pertento's last attempts at salvaging a belief in a being greater than the physical realm.

"How old are the results?" I asked.

"The tests were conducted in 2404."

Fifteen years ago. I had been seven. Old enough to recall if I'd been poked and prodded in a lab, with blood drawn and my brain scanned. And yet I couldn't remember a single moment. Not the face of my doctor, or the fluorescent white lights that would have flooded my vision. Things that I *should* have remembered.

My heart was roaring in my ears as my heart pumped harder in my chest, fighting to supply my heaving lungs with enough oxygen to keep from fainting. Why couldn't I remember?

"Are you sure?" I asked in between gasps. My lungs ached.

Klara crouched down on the floor in front of me, taking my hands. "Squeeze," she ordered. "Squeeze my hands. Focus on my face. *Breathe*."

Flexing my fingers, I squeezed Klara's hands. Gently at first, and then harder as my body fought against my lungs in an all-out war. Despite the white spots that blurred my vision, I managed to search Klara's face: the depth of her brow, the upturn of her nose, the freckles above her top lip. As I studied the details, the white melted away, my vision stabilizing.

"You're in control," Klara said. The words echoed in my head as though bouncing around in my skull.

Something snapped together inside me, and I inhaled sharply. My lungs surrendered themselves to me once again, and it was only a minute before I was able to catch my breath.

"You're the same person you were yesterday," Klara reminded me, still crouched at my feet and looking up at my face through dark lashes. "What you know now is only as scary as you allow it to be."

"What do I do now?"

Before Klara could answer, there was a loud mumbling from somewhere across the infirmary. I followed the sound, which led me to spot Silens, who was fast asleep in one of the infirmary's beds. Until then, I'd almost forgotten how he'd collapsed and started to seize under my touch.

I shot Klara a desperate look. "Did I do that to him?"

"Not on purpose. Though he's refusing to accept it, he is also inhuman. He's developed his ability later in life, like you have, and his senses are elevated by emotion. I suspect that when you two came in contact, there was an adverse reaction between your two abilities. His ability was enhanced to a level that was incompatible with his body, causing him to seize."

I bit my lip, watching Silens as he rolled over onto his side, his face turned toward us. Unbothered.

"I'm dangerous, then?"

"I don't believe so," Klara answered. "When we come into our abilities, we have no control over them, meaning that they'll become active as a natural response to fear or extreme emotion. In your case, Quercus scared you. And with them butting heads, it only heightened your fear, activating your ability."

"And Silens?"

Klara giggled. "He's got a big heart, but a short temper."

I glanced at my hands, still interlocked in Klara's. "I won't hurt you?"

Klara released my hands, holding them up. "I'm still wearing gloves. If my theory is correct, your ability would only interfere with others' abilities through skin-to-skin contact, if at all."

Tucking my hands into my lap, I folded my fingers together. Though my ability, whatever it was, would remain dormant so long as I kept my emotions in check, I didn't trust myself enough to have my hands on another person. I startled too easily. I'd been there less than a day, and I'd already caused more than enough trouble because of my inability to keep my emotions under wraps.

Klara nudged my knee. "He'll be fine," she assured. "When he wakes up, he might have a bit of a headache, but, otherwise, he's healthy."

"Does anybody else know about…?"

"About your ability?" Klara asked, as though reading my mind.

She had a knack for that, I had begun to realize. If Alessandra hadn't already told me about Klara's ability, I might have guessed that she was a telepath. She always seemed to know what others were about to say or what they needed to hear.

I guess she's just good at reading people.

"Everybody knows that your ability is on the fifth tier," Alessandra answered for her.

So that was why everyone had been shooting me wary glances, the tougher among them seeming even more hostile than the others.

Klara gave Alessandra a glare that carried the weight of a hundred words. Only the words were in a language that I failed to understand.

"*But,* only those of you who were present in that room—myself included—know about the incident with Treyton," Klara added.

On the other side of the room, Silens shifted again in his sleep, resting his cheek on top of his arm. I searched his face for any signs of discomfort, but there was only a small smile tugging at his lips as he slept.

"Why do you call him Treyton?" I asked.

Klara's eyes gravitated toward Silens' side of the room. "I've known him for a long time," she answered simply. Though I had achieved no deeper understanding, I decided to leave that question be for a little while longer.

"You said he's an inhuman?"

"His recent behaviour leads me to believe he is," Klara said. "The results for the test that I ran should be in within a couple of hours,

and then I'll have the proof to confirm it."

"But you're not certain?"

Klara gave a short, nasally laugh. It would have been a startling reaction if it weren't for the warmth in the rich green and brown of her eyes.

"I started apprenticing for this position twelve years ago, and I've known Treyton since we were old enough to peer over the dinner table. I don't need a test to tell me what I already know."

"You said you believed. Belief isn't certainty."

A strand of hair had escaped the hold of her elastic, and Klara tucked it behind her ear. She scooped up the file still resting on the foot of the bed. "Just because you know something for certain doesn't mean you can't also believe that it's true."

I refrained from wrinkling my nose at the concept. What was the point in believing in something when you already had the facts lined up in front of you? If you laid out a mathematical sequence that totalled correctly *and* believed it to be correct, what could you possibly gain? The sequence wouldn't become *more* correct.

"You've had a long day," Klara said, yanking me from my thoughts. "Feel free to rest your head."

"Wait."

A question was gnawing at my brain, and I worried that if I went to sleep, I'd lose it.

"You said that the Ascendancy should have known about my..." I hesitated. "About my inhumanity, by now. So why didn't they? Why aren't I dead?"

Klara's shoulders sank, her face contorting. "I was hoping that you'd know the answer. I'll have to dig deeper into your files and put a timeline together, but if we're missing a piece to your puzzle, I can guarantee you that I won't rest until I find it. Believe me."

I nodded, glancing back up at the blank display. My reflection stared back at me on the black screen. If only the answers to the

questions I had could have presented themselves through the display, we'd all have been saved from the trouble of a search.

A search that did not guarantee answers, unlike Klara was promising.

Promises were empty until they were filled. And from my experience, you'd have an easier time filling a bottomless hole in the earth with a salad fork.

SEVENTEEN

SILENS

THE HUMMING ACHE IN TREYTON'S FOREHEAD stirred him from his sleep. When his eyes cracked open, they drank in the white LED lighting, bright spots dancing across his vision. Carefully lifting himself up into a sitting position against the headboard, he craned his neck to search the room.

The infirmary.

How did I get here?

Last he remembered, he was looking down on Quercus, heat beating against his face as he fought the urge to bury his knuckles into the other man's jaw.

On the opposite side of the room, Miles was curled up on top of one of the beds, the sheets unbothered beneath her.

Drawing the covers up around his bare arms, Treyton wondered if she was cold. If it wasn't for the way his limbs groaned, he might have made his way over to that end of the room to pull the covers over the top of her.

At the thought of her well-being, he remembered.

Quercus had gotten too close to her, wrapping his arms around her and holding her still. Restraining her, despite her protests. Treyton remembered the anxiety in her face as Quercus had approached her, and the way she'd fought against his body despite being far too small to fend him off herself. All of it flooded back to Treyton now in jagged waves. The memory alone was enough to send his heart racing again, a buzzing sound in his ears.

Treyton could admit that he was impulsive. He spoke his mind and would be the first to put up a fight for no plausible reason other than to see the authoritative figures in his life, like his fathers or James, squirm. But he was no hero. So why had he been trying so hard to be one?

When it came to her and her safety, Treyton was beginning to notice a trend: He saw nothing but red. It was an impulse out of his control. And it was just as much a mystery to him as it was anyone else.

Pulling his hand out from under the covers, he examined it, turning it over and giving his fingers a wiggle. Miles had grabbed him by the hand before the world around him had given way to darkness, only for him to wake up in the infirmary. Resting his hand in his lap, his eyes wandered back over to the Ascendant woman.

But the opening and closing of a door wrestled his attention to the other end of the room, where Klara had emerged from behind her office doors.

"Good morning, sunshine," she said. Klara moved to stand at the foot of his bed, scribbling something onto her clipboard.

"What year is it?" Treyton asked, only partly joking.

"Relax," she said. "You've only been out for nine hours."

"Best nine hours of my life."

Klara snorted. A soft, delicate kind of snort.

Treyton's lips twitched into a grin. He gestured to Miles—still sound asleep—with a nod of his head. "She's okay?"

"She was detained, but once Alessandra convinced her groupies that she wasn't a threat to anyone, they both came here."

Treyton nodded his head, still studying Miles' sleeping face. Even from across the room, he could see the flutter of her eyelids as she grew immersed in a dream. Or a nightmare.

"She fell asleep waiting for you to wake up," Klara said, the tip of her pen falling still against the page she'd been writing on.

"They haven't assigned her sleeping arrangements yet?"

Klara glanced Miles' way. "I'm sure they have. But I think she wanted to apologize to you. She feels guilty about what happened."

Regret wrapped its ready hand around his heart and gave it a squeeze. His memories were still foggy, and he was still uncertain about how he had ended up in the infirmary rather than in his own room. Whatever had happened, he couldn't imagine Miles being at fault. There didn't seem to be a fighting bone in her body, never mind the intention of putting someone in harm's way.

"Do you remember what happened?" Klara asked, resuming her pen-scribbling.

Treyton shook his head. "Just that I was about to knock the lights out of that D-bag, and now I'm here."

Klara circled around to flank the side of his bed, retrieving a small flashlight from another pocket of her coat. When she shone it into his eyes, he jolted back against his pillow.

"So what's your issue with the guy, anyway? Alessandra tells me that you were at his throat the second he walked into the room."

Unable to tolerate the light beating against his corneas, Treyton pushed the flashlight away with a gentle hand. "You don't find it the least bit suspicious?"

A sparkle in her eye betrayed her amusement. "That you seem to have an issue with any male that walks into the room? The damage to your boyish ego isn't exactly on my list of concerns, Ton."

He wrinkled his nose at that. "This isn't about me, it's about Quercus. Until tonight, I didn't even know the guy existed."

"Technically, last night," she corrected him, pointing her thumb toward the clock on the wall near the infirmary entrance.

If his head were not throbbing as though it had been split down the middle, he might have been in the mood to tease her about her incessant need to correct him. For now, though, he decided to let her have this one and settled for a half-hearted glare.

"How important do you think you are that you'd know *everybody*?" she continued.

"You're not listening," Treyton growled, growing more frustrated.

Klara's jaw twitched. Now he had done it.

"By all means, enlighten me," she retorted.

Great. Now I've pissed her off.

He cleared his throat. "Like I was saying, I've never seen the guy. Am I just supposed to believe that he is who they say he is?"

By the way the lighter-brown flecks in her eyes dimmed, he could tell that Klara's patience was starting to grow thin.

Treyton began to wonder how long she'd been awake. Had she been up all this time, monitoring him? That would mean that Miles hadn't been the only one waiting on him. And now that he was finally awake, he had been talking her ear off. It was something she would normally have no problem tolerating, but it was the brink of morning, and it didn't appear that she'd gotten a wink of sleep. Even though they—the Resiliens—lived underground, deprived of the sun's schedule, people's bodies had adapted over time to regulate their sleep patterns. And Klara's had been disturbed big-time.

"You know what?" he said, lowering himself back into bed. "I'm exhausted."

"You just slept for nine hours and you're tired?" She regarded him with her brows drawn together, her gaze burning metaphorical holes into his face. Like she was picking him apart and unravelling every fibre of his being.

Brilliant, Treyton. Just brilliant. Scrap together a few more brain cells and lie a little smarter, would you?

Treyton expected her to call him out, but was surprised when she only nodded her head. "All right, then," she said. "We'll talk more about this later." She leaned forward, brushing his hair back to leave a kiss so soft against his forehead that her lips hardly grazed his skin. "Goodnight, Ton."

"Goodnight," he said, watching as she moved across the room to shut off the lights before slipping into her office again.

Turning over onto his side, Treyton wrapped the covers tighter around his body, willing himself back to sleep. After a half an hour of staring at the blank canvas of the wall, the lulling silence brought him to slumber's doorstep.

When he blinked open his eyes, the clock read half past ten.

A faint knock at the entrance doors drew his eyes toward that end of the room. Who would knock on the infirmary doors rather than just walking in? The infirmary was a public space between the hours of eight a.m. and nine p.m., after all.

Before he could draw the covers back to go see who was behind the odd knocking, Klara was scurrying across the room, gathering her hair in both hands as she pulled it into a quick ponytail. Gluing a smile to her face, she swung one door open readily.

The two—Klara and whoever it was on the other side of the door—exchanged hushed whispers. It was a quick conversation. Whoever it was must've had a question.

Treyton wondered what the question was or what had been said between them. If it was such a private subject, it must have been urgent.

"Have a nice day," Klara whispered, easing the door closed.

"What was that about?" he called as he swung his feet over the edge of the bed, laying his bare feet flat against the ground. The cool floor against his skin sent small shocks through his legs.

Klara gave a start. "I didn't realize you were awake."

"Did you get any sleep?" Treyton asked, reaching over his shoulder to massage an ache in his neck.

What the hell had happened yesterday that his entire body was achy, with a constant drumming in his head? No matter how he fought to remember, the thick, dark fog that plagued his memory persisted.

"Not much," Klara admitted. "But duty calls." She snuck him one of her radiant smiles.

His stomach tightened. He had been neglecting duties of his own. Every day that passed, the threat of the Ascendancy grew nearer. It brewed stronger, like a hurricane fueled by the rapid rise of warm, humid air. Only instead of warm air, the motives of the Ascendancy were driven by unrelenting discrimination and mindless control.

And there he was, lying in bed. Wasting time. Every hour that he spent getting his beauty rest, young children who might not live to experience the light of the sun against their youthful shoulders were at risk. Families were praying at their bedsides, and the elderly were mourning the joy of their earlier, freer years.

Collecting his boots from where they'd been left at the foot of his bed, Treyton began to pull them on, yanking the laces as tight as they would go.

"Where do you think you're going?" Klara interrogated, moving to block the path between him and the exit.

"Out."

As he lifted himself to his feet, warmth exploded in his chest cavity. It seeped into his bones, easing the stiffness that he had awoken to.

But when Klara lifted her wrist to his forehead, as though to check his temperature, the intensity of the warmth grew stronger until he could hardly bear the sensation.

Grinding his teeth against the burning that pulsated throughout his body, Treyton regarded her with wide, panicked eyes. "Something's wrong."

Klara's lips curved into a sympathetic frown. "Ton…"

"What's wrong with me?" he spat, resentful of the compassion in her gaze.

Klara took a step backward, taken aback by his outburst, no doubt. "You need to calm down and listen to me."

"Calm down? You want me to calm down?! I'm burning, Klara!"

The sensation was unnatural.

Inhuman.

"Just make it stop," he pleaded. Every nerve in his body raged with fire, his own breath hot against his lips as he panted.

Treyton threw himself back onto the mattress, gripping the hair on his head and pulling, hard. Anything to distract him from his suffering.

"I can't stop it," she said. "And you know that. You need to try and control it."

"I can't!"

"*Try*." The word came out like a cry from her trembling lips.

How was he supposed to control something that he barely understood? *Couldn't* understand?

What Treyton understood now, though, was what she had been trying to tell him all this time; what he had suspected since his body had started acting unusually. Yet, even if all the signs pointed toward it, his stubbornness would never allow him to admit defeat over the very thing that currently held a flame to every cell in his body.

Shaking his head, he grabbed at his shirt, tugging it over his head and throwing it to the floor. "Water," he gasped.

No. Scratch that.

"Ice, *please*."

Klara's expression changed. Pity seized her face as he grimaced in front of her, bent over in agony. Watching him must have been like watching an injured animal that hobbled along the side of the road.

Her eyes were wet. Empathy was what made her a good doctor. He could see that this was hurting her, maybe even more than it was hurting him.

Without another word, she spun around and rushed for the infirmary doors, disappearing behind them.

The heat had spread to Treyton's fingertips. Everything he touched only amplified the fire raging in his veins. Multiples of his vision were dancing around him; the walls swayed from side to side; the ground dipped in places around the room.

I'm dying, he thought. *I have to be.*

It was a possibility. There had been several cases in which the inhuman had been killed by their abilities.

In one case, a young girl had come into her ability—to produce electricity from her fingertips—too early. At only twelve years old, developing more rapidly than her small vessel could contain, her ability had electrocuted her from the inside out, completely frying her internal organs.

Scorched her heart to black.

The thought sent Treyton's stomach into a somersault.

A stab in his abdomen made him cry out. He cradled his stomach in his hands, grinding his teeth so hard that his gums ached in his mouth.

Please, God, make it stop.

EIGHTEEN

SILENS

HANDS GRASPED HIS SHOULDERS, holding him upright.

Thank God, Treyton thought, reaching up to touch Klara's face. Yet, when he looked up through his lashes, he only found Miles' deep eyes looking steadily into his own, her hands soft against his skin.

Taking a short breath, he tore himself away from her, slumping back against the mattress. "Don't burn yourself," he managed to warn her in between drawn-out gasps.

She quirked her lips. "Where's Klara?" she asked.

As if the God he had prayed to since he was a child had heard his plea, the heat gave way, receding from Treyton's body as quickly as it had come. His every muscle quivered, weak with exertion, and his chest heaved. Nevertheless, he welcomed the relief with a heavy sigh.

Thank you.

Miles stood at his bedside with wide eyes, stunned. "What's wrong with you?"

How delicate of her. He wondered if she'd approach a terminally ill patient in that same manner.

"Puberty," he remarked, shutting his eyes.

His head still throbbed, and the last thing he wanted to do was have a conversation about this. Even though he was fairly certain what "this" was, he didn't want to put it into words. Because if he said it aloud, it would be a reality. And sometimes putting off reality was easier than admitting it was swallowing you whole.

Miles narrowed her eyes. "You told me not to burn myself, but on what? Did something burn you?"

"Do you always ask so many dumb questions?" he asked, peeking one eye open at her.

"Why can't you give me a straight answer?" she countered, folding her arms and tilting her head to one side.

Treyton bit back the remark dangling at the end of his tongue, shutting his eyes again. It wouldn't be fair of him to fault her for wanting answers. If he were in her shoes, he would be asking just as many questions, if not more. Not that he would be caught dead in her shoes. They weren't his colour.

Wait a minute, he thought. Every square inch of him had been red-hot. How could she not have felt that?

Sitting upright, gripping the edge of the bed with both hands to hold himself upright, still weak from his attack, Treyton regarded her with probing eyes.

"Didn't you feel it?"

"Feel what?"

He searched her eyes for evidence of deception or amusement but came up short. Her oblivion was sincere. She should have been able to feel the heat of his skin, like an intense fever, at the least.

What did that mean? Was he experiencing anything real at all, or was his brain playing tricks on him? He put his face in his hands.

It's official. I've lost it.

Hurried footsteps alerted them to someone entering the room, and Treyton lifted his head.

Klara approached. She gripped a file in her hands, the paper wrinkling under the pressure of her grasp.

"Thank you for taking your time," Treyton said, careful to keep his tone lighthearted to prevent their earlier argument from resurfacing. "Could you please explain to me what the hell is going on before I wind up cooking an egg on my chest?"

The two women's eyes fell to his bare chest for a second before they redirected their gazes elsewhere, flushes of pink colouring their cheeks. He pretended not to notice.

"Tier-two ability," Klara said with ease, as though the three words didn't carry any weight to them.

Treyton's fingers felt numb as he took the file, which she held out to him, and began to flip through the pages inside. And there it was, staring back at him in black and white. As official as his certification of birth.

He was inhuman.

A scream bubbled in his chest, but he kept his composure, aware that Miles was studying him with her dark eyes. She was also inhuman and must have held a predisposed bias against her—*their*—own subspecies. The news was just as fresh in her mind as it was in his despite his earlier suspicions, which Klara had planted in his mind to begin with.

Even if Treyton didn't know where he stood currently in his fathers' plans, there was one thing he could be certain about. She *was* the key, just as they had said. A point of reference. Without her, there would be no revolution. No redemption for people like her.

For people like him.

Miles was timid, skittish. Even the slightest of movements startled her away from acceptance of her situation. But every so often, a spark seemed to ignite in her that equipped her tongue and fueled a passionate fire within her. A fire that must have been snuffed out time and time again. When she shed her Ascendant skin, she became her whole self. Not the shell of a human being that Murus had trained her to be.

Treyton saw that, even if nobody else would. And if he reacted to the confirmation of his inhumanity based on his own sentiments, he would startle her; send her fleeing as far as her short legs would take her. He refused to be added to the list of people who had snuffed out her flame.

"I know that it's not what you want to hear, but once you come to accept it, you can start to control it. Your attacks will get less severe, and you'll..."

Klara's voice tapered off as his mind wandered elsewhere, trailing toward Miles and the predicament she'd been caught in.

Her entire life had been uprooted and replanted in an entirely different soil, and was now deprived of the elements on which it used to thrive. Her leaves were beginning to wilt at the edges. Her faith wavered. Treyton could see it in the way she questioned everyone and everything around her. He wondered if she'd ever known certainty or maintained beliefs of her own. Beliefs that were hers and not the word of law.

Even her resolve was lacking. Despite her questions, she was finding no answers. And rather than putting up a fight and taking those answers for herself, she backed down. Submitted to the strange and unfamiliar world around her.

He knew firsthand about the internal battles she was facing. At an earlier point in his life, he had preferred to lay low. To go with the flow of things as they came. But that was only until he had gotten caught beneath his brother's shadow. Then he'd had no choice.

If he didn't fight his own battles, his brother certainly wasn't going to be the one to do it for him.

"Ton, are you listening to me? Before you start having one of your meltdowns—"

"I'm okay," Treyton said, cutting her short. "Why am I here, again?"

A shadow of guilt flickered over Miles' taut expression, and he frowned.

Klara furrowed her brow, looking unconvinced. "Okay..." she said, the word laced with suspicion.

Treyton lowered his eyes, careful not to catch her probing gaze.

"Newly developed abilities can be unpredictable and hard to control. Until the ability develops further and you're able to manipulate it, it can be hard to tell just how different abilities might interact with one another. When you and Miles made physical contact, her ability intensified yours, which caused you to seize because of your body's inability to contain the doubled, possibly tripled, strength of your ability. Luckily, that big head of yours didn't take any neurological damage."

Miles snorted, and Treyton almost missed the soft red glow on the high points of her cheeks as she brought her hands up to cover her mouth and nose, turning her eyes away. He suppressed the twitch in his lips, which threatened a grin.

"So as long as Miles can control herself around me—and I know that must be difficult, given my dashing good looks and all—my brain won't explode?"

"I think you're giving yourself too much credit, mister," Miles retorted.

There it was. A speck of gold illuminated her dark eyes, but only for a heartbeat.

Well played, he thought.

"New abilities tend to flare up in circumstances of extreme emotion, like fear or grief," Klara continued, "so you'll be fine as long as Miles' emotions are stable. In the meantime"—Klara turned to Miles—"you'll need to wear gloves and be sure to avoid skin-to-skin contact with anyone, just to be safe. Sound good?"

Miles nodded her agreement.

"While I'm at it, let me find you a change of clothes, too," Klara said, looking Miles' current attire up and down before whirling on her heels and scurrying into her office.

"What's wrong with what I'm wearing?" Miles asked him, looking pleasantly offended.

Treyton examined her clothing. The entire ensemble was white. It would be easy to pick her out amongst them in those clothes, which were obviously Ascendant-wear. Not that she was making any effort to hide her status as an outsider. They had thrown her into this mess, giving her little to no say. But now that she was here, there was no turning back.

No going home.

"Nothing."

That much was true. Though the white was obnoxious and just another reminder of the Ascendancy's absurd and unfair values, the colour suited her. It brought her pale skin to life and accentuated her dark hair where it spilled down around her shoulders.

"You just stand out like a sore thumb wearing that around here," he said. "People'll stare."

"Like you know anything about people staring," she muttered.

"I do." The words came out sharper than he had intended, and she flinched. Treyton tried to shrug off the wave of guilt that crashed over him.

They stood in silence until Klara returned, hugging a pile of clothing to her chest—a standard Arxwoman's uniform. Atop the pile was a pair of black gloves.

After handing the clothes to Miles and guiding her into her office to change, Klara returned to take her spot next to Treyton on the bed. She bit her lip, analyzing his face.

"What are you looking at?"

"You sure you're okay?" she asked, resting a hand on his knee.

"You threw a fit and stormed out of here yesterday."

A good question. One he didn't have a concise enough answer for. He had spent his entire life fighting on behalf of the inhuman—what could be considered an act of selflessness. Something his fathers would say that he ought to do more of.

Should he fall into the hands of the Ascendancy, God forbid, he knew that even if he didn't leave much to his name, he would be proud to have been on the right side of wrong. While there wasn't much else he was able to do, protecting those who couldn't protect themselves had become a practice he didn't have to think twice about. But what he knew about his inhumanity changed all of that.

Rather than being the protector, he was the one in need of a guardian angel, somebody to watch *his* back when he was too busy to watch his own. Lord knew he couldn't depend on his brother for that, nor his parents. If it came down to a choice between him and James, Treyton knew that his parents would side with his older brother, not necessarily because they favoured him but because they pitied him.

Treyton's inhumanity was out of his control, yet he couldn't help but think he was being greedy, as though his inhumanity were an illness he could have prevented somehow. But that was foolish. It wasn't like it sat beneath his nails in a layer of grime, just waiting to be scrubbed away.

"Ton?"

Treyton lifted his chin. "Right as rain," he answered her finally.

Over the years, the two of them had entrusted each other with many secrets and emotional confessionals. But those words were all he could muster.

He was no better than any citizen of the Ascendancy, because the very knowledge of his inhumanity made his skin crawl. Shame ripped him apart from the inside out, because as much as he hated to admit it, even if just to himself, a small sliver of him was unsettled.

And though it was only a fraction of his attitude, that fraction carried a powerful punch.

More than anything, he was terrified. To wake up one day and be someone you weren't—or rather, never had been—was far from reassuring. When there was someone you disliked, you could avoid them. You could leave the room, or otherwise keep from making contact. When you were afraid of something, you could work around the object or entity from which that fear originated.

But when you were afraid of yourself? There was no escaping or avoiding that fear. You woke up, and there it was, staring back at you with dark, ravenous caverns for eyes, ready to consume you.

Squeezing his knee, Klara wrestled him away from the brigade of his anxieties with one gesture. Falling into the still, greenish-brown depths of her familiar gaze, the tension that had been squeezing the air from his lungs eased.

The door to Klara's office cracked open, and Miles poked her head out.

"I look ridiculous."

"We'll be the judge of that." Klara beckoned her out of the room with a wave of her hand.

After hesitating and disappearing again behind the shelter of the office door, Miles faltered into view. The dark material of the uniform bunched around her shoulders as she cradled her abdomen in her arms. Unlike her Ascendant getup, this uniform was skin-tight, hugging every curve of her form.

It fit perfectly with the exception of the sleeves, which were a touch too short. The anthene textile was ribbed on the knees and elbows, allowing for easy movement. And though the uniform was almost entirely black, it was accented by silver thread sewn into the collar and barrel cuffs in a feathery pattern. And on her hands she wore black gloves.

Simple.

Safe.

"I look like an idiot," Miles said, tugging at the fabric around her thighs.

Treyton gave her a once-over. She didn't look half bad. But she did look uncomfortable: slumped shoulders, with loose locks of her dark hair curtaining her downcast face. It was almost difficult to watch—her trying to cover up as much as she could, allowing her posture to sag as she wrapped her arms around herself.

She has to be the least confident person I've ever known.

"That's nonsense. Idiots wear all sorts of clothing," he countered, willing to press a nerve if it meant coercing some hint of self-assurance out of her.

The gazes of both women bored into his skin as they turned to glower at him.

Despite being the target of their frustrations, a glimmer of hope sparked in his chest because, for the first time since changing into the Resiliens uniform, Miles' spark returned. She straightened her shoulders and pursed her lips together as she regarded him with fiery disbelief.

That's it. Defend yourself, he thought. *Fight back, kiddo.*

But the spark flickered out again, and she turned away, letting her arms dangle at her sides. It was as though she'd been drained completely of life. Of retaliation. Even Klara, the most patient woman he had known to date, had her moments of unbridled defiance.

What am I going to do with you, Amissa?

NINETEEN

SILENS

"WHAT HAPPENS NOW?" He asked once Miles was out of earshot, on her way to relieve herself in the infirmary's restroom. It would only be a few minutes before she returned, which left him and Klara with little time for private discussion.

"Well, we'll have to wait until you both develop further into your abilities enough to somewhat identify them before either of you can begin your training."

Klara was stripping the bed he had slept in of its sheets while he watched, sure to keep out of her way. Treyton knew better than to interfere with her job. She was a stickler for perfection. Everything had to be in order, or the disturbance would become a distraction, like a persistent ache in her ear.

"I meant about her."

Reaching up into the cupboard on the back of the wall, Klara retrieved a clean set of sheets and set them down on the bare mattress. "She has a name, y'know."

Aiming a finger at her, Treyton feigned a reprimanding snarl, which she responded to with a roll of her eyes.

"Why are you asking me? My work doesn't exceed those doors," she said, gesturing toward the infirmary exit with a nod of her head.

The lie, whether intentional or otherwise, nipped at his heart. She was involved, perhaps in ways she didn't even realize. Collecting information about a girl—an Ascendant girl, no less—made it seem like she was pretty involved in something that "exceeded" her work.

Klara unfolded the linen before she began tucking the bottom sheet underneath the edges of the mattress.

"Why don't you ask your parents?" she continued. "They're responsible for anyone that comes in or out of this base."

Treyton would be all right if he never heard from his parents again. Not because he didn't love them, but because they were his superiors. So long as they ranked above him, their jobs as department heads overruled their jobs as parents.

When children grow older and more independent of their parents, they require space. Time alone; time to be their own individuals. But when your parents were your bosses, there was no escaping them. Whether Treyton liked it or not, they were aware of his every movement, because they had to be. Not out of concern or genuine interest, but because his existence impacted the nature of their work.

"You think my parents trust me enough to tell what their master plan is?"

The question was rhetorical. In the years he and Klara had known one another, she had never once bad-mouthed his fathers. When they were kids, it had been a matter of respect. They were their elders, and, as children, they had been brought up to respect their elders.

But now, it was because she was playing it safe. They were her employers, not just two older men that she happened to know through their son. And it didn't take a genius to understand that speaking poorly about one's employer behind their back could result in termination. Klara loved her work too much to defend even him and risk the career she'd built for herself.

Pinching her brow together, a look of warning passed over Klara's expression. Her hands lingered over the top bedsheet as she lowered her voice.

"This isn't a matter of trust, Treyton. This is a matter of life and death and the safety of everybody here."

He stared down at his feet, regret pulling his stomach into a knot. When reprimand came from his parents or his brother, he was able to shrug off the sternness of their tones without so much as a second thought. With her, though, the words carried the weight of a thousand punches.

When it became clear to her that her reprimand had brought him back down to earth, her expression softened, as did her tone.

"The world isn't out to get you, and neither are your parents. Stop making them out to be the villains. You owe Miles that much. I don't know if you've noticed, but Daddy Amissa isn't exactly on Santa's nice list."

Treyton snorted at her reference to the old children's myth. Such holidays hadn't been celebrated in over a century. But Klara had always had a soft spot for old familial traditions. Every year, she would rope him into ringing in the new year with her, the two of them perched at the end of her bed as they reflected on the days gone by.

On the lessons learned.

Memories made.

The practice was cheesy, and Treyton was always sure to make that known through his teasing, which he would mutter under his breath. But he knew that she heard it anyway, just as she knew that was just the way he would always be. They accepted one another for who the other was without any reservations.

"They pulled one over even on James. I'd say they have a plan," she said.

Pulling the final corner of the top sheet over the mattress, she took a step back to admire her handiwork. "Put a little faith in them, and maybe they'll pay it forward. You're their son. They're strict on you because they know more about your potential than you think."

Treyton scraped at the ground with the toe of his boot. "So you're not concerned?"

"About?" she asked, elevating a brow.

"Their intentions. With Miles."

"What's there to be concerned about? They've offered her a refuge. A roof over her head. What would they have to gain from scheming something?"

He reclaimed his spot on the foot of the bed, wrinkling the sheet. The twitch in Klara's cheek encouraged a brief, apologetic smile from him.

"Think about it," he urged. "She's supposed to be the key, right? But why? Because she's Murus' daughter? That doesn't seem like enough of a reason to lure her here and try to convince her to take our side. We're just lucky she's gullible."

Klara's expression shifted. But what was it that seeped into the cracks of her forced smile? Sympathy?

Whatever it was, it seemed he had hit a nerve, somehow.

Turning his words over in his mind, Treyton realized that they were rather insensitive. But he dismissed the sliver of guilt that nagged him.

"I don't have the answers you're looking for," Klara said, shooing him off the bed and smoothing the sheet under her palms. "And keep off these, would you? I'll never get this place in order if you keep acting like you're entitled to every square inch."

He widened his eyes, covering his gaping mouth with a hand, putting on a show of shock.

"You mean…I'm not?"

A victim of his charms, the corners of Klara's lips curled upward into a faint smile. When she noticed him watching her morphing expression, she turned her back to him, reaching up into the cupboard overhead again. She riffled through its contents for something, only to turn up empty-handed.

"What's taking that girl so long?" Klara asked, peering over her shoulder and casting a glance toward the washroom. Closing the stretch of distance between them and the door in a few skips, Klara taped her knuckles against the thin steel. "Everything all right in there?"

The voice that responded was low, almost inaudible to Treyton from where he stood. "I just need a minute."

Pity.

That was what he had recognized earlier in Klara's expression. Judging by the way her bottom lip protruded from its companion, the sentiment was planning an encore. It was a gesture that would have been easily missed by the untrained eye. Luckily for him, he had spent every day for the last fifteen years studying her face and the way her expressions correlated with the inner workings of her emotional mind. She experienced empathy for Miles, and it was easy to understand why.

Unlike himself, Klara had been a registered Ascendant citizen, now thought to be dead in the eyes of the Ascendancy. And even without having her ability as company in her earlier, formative years, memories from the past life she'd lived were built on a foundation of ignorance, hatred, and force.

Of being deprived of her voice; of her ability to speak and stand up for her rights.

If anyone could relate to Miles and try to break through to her, it would be Klara.

Treyton's fathers had given Miles a decision to make. Or, at least, they believed they had. But blackmail and false endangerment hardly seemed like giving someone much of a choice to him.

If living under the Ascendancy could even be recognized as a life. Every move someone made, every decision, right down to who they were allowed to spend their leisure hours with within the schoolyard, was predetermined.

Calculated.

Maybe the choice wasn't determining where her loyalties lay, but having the ability to decide.

A decision for or against freedom.

Life.

A choice that could provide free speech and self-respect.

But what did his parents want with Miles, really? Why her?

Sure, she was Murus' daughter. But from what he had gathered so far, the two of them didn't have much of a relationship at all. She was scared of everything, and it wouldn't have surprised him if Murus was the reason why. Those who respected Murus wouldn't dare to cross him. One act of defiance from a young Miles, and Treyton could only imagine the terrors she must have seen.

Witnessed.

Maybe even experienced.

His skin crawled at the thought that maybe she carried not only emotional, psychological scars, but physical scars that transcribed a history of physical abuse.

The father-and-daughter duo were about as tight-knit as he was with his brother. James was many things, but even he couldn't hold a candle to that Amissa man in the department of being a grade-A jerk. James certainly was a jackass, but not enough of one to manipulate thousands of people and orchestrate a terrorist attack upon his own citizens.

"So, are we going to talk about your obvious fascination with her?"

Treyton straightened up. "Huh?"

"With Miles," Klara clarified. "You haven't peeled your eyes away from her since she got here. And when you can't keep an eye on her like some love-crazed hawk, it's all you can stand to talk about."

"That's a bit of a reach."

"Is it? You just tried to pit me against your parents with a loose claim that you have no hard evidence to support. You're grasping at loose ends, trying to prove an unnecessary suspicion, all because you're trying to protect her. I just can't figure out why yet."

He ran a hand through his dishevelled hair. "Does there have to be a reason? It's literally my job to protect people."

"Even so, you've been acting...not yourself, since she's started wandering these tunnels."

"Not myself?"

Had he been acting strangely? He hardly thought so. As far as he could tell, he was himself as usual. Dashing, quick on his feet, and a sight for sore eyes, if he had anything to say about it. Maybe a little cockier than usual, but that was only because he was having a good day. Save for the whole "there's a maniacal dictator trying to kill me and all of my loved ones" thing.

For once, the eyes weren't on him. They were on *her*.

Miles.

He swallowed. Had she been overtaking his thoughts after all?

Shaking his head, he dismissed the thought. Of course she had. She was a stranger. A threat. Maybe not a direct threat, but a connection to a very real, very dangerous threat. He had every right to have his mind on her. Everybody else did.

"You attacked Quercus," Klara said, still staring at him, her eyes threatening to burn holes into his own. "You're annoying, but you're not a violent person."

"He deserved it!" he exclaimed, fighting to defend himself despite his better judgement. Then, raising his voice a little, he hissed through his teeth, "You weren't even there."

Klara stole a quick glance toward the exit. Her way of warning him that if he didn't wisen up, she'd have every right to have him escorted away.

"I'm doing my job," Treyton continued, leaning against the bed again. "That's all. And as somebody that's doing their job, I think that there's more to all of this than my parents are letting on."

Klara threw up her hands, turning her back on him. Perhaps circling back to his conspiracies wasn't the best provocation to drive his part of the debate forward, after all.

When she turned to face him again, she rushed forward, hurrying him away from the bed with frantic waves of her hands. Amusement seized hold of Treyton's lips, twisting them into a mischievous smirk of satisfaction.

"Let's pretend for a moment that I understand what you're getting at here," she said, tangling her fingers in his and guiding him over to the front desk, where she made him sit in her chair rather than on her fresh linen. Leaning her hip into the edge of the desk, she withdrew her hands and hid them away in her coat pockets. "Are you saying that you think your parents are using Miles?"

"She's the only fifth-tier inhuman but has no knowledge of her ability or the power she might possess. My fathers are using her as leverage, but as far as I can tell, she's about as valuable to Murus and the Ascendancy as pork to a horse."

Klara wrinkled her nose. A bad metaphor, he knew, but he had never claimed to be a man of literary prowess.

"What ulterior motive could they have for bringing her here, then, do you think?"

Treyton dragged a hand over his face, tilting his head upward in thought. "I'm worried that they wanna weaponize her."

A flickering light illuminated Klara's round eyes. "If you're right, then your parents have lost their minds. If we use our abilities as weapons against the Ascendancy, we'd only be confirming every theory they've publicized about our kind."

The word *our* resonated with him heavier than it had before. The Resiliens was a family. A united front. But with the confirmation of his inhumanity came a wry sense of inclusivity—something he would have given anything for when he was a kid, but loathed in his adulthood.

The world had shut him up, backing him into the corner that he would come to call his own. He had learned to embrace his individuality—his isolation—even going as far as to jump up on tables and scream at the top of his lungs if he so desired, all to keep himself set apart. That was what everyone wanted, and he would have hated to disappoint his audience.

"I'm going to keep an eye on her," Treyton said. "Try not to get too jealous."

Klara, who was rummaging through one of her desk drawers, looked up at him through her dark lashes. "I wouldn't dream of it." Straightening up, she rested her hand atop his head. "Just be careful, Ton."

He tilted his head, squinting his eyes in question.

"Miles is a gentle soul, which you gravitate toward. But you can't let your relationship with her compromise the Resiliens' purpose."

As she took her hand from his head and held it against his chest, Treyton gave a smile made only for her. "Don't worry about me. I want to look out for her because we're both outcasts, and I owe her that much. But that's all that's going on."

Freeing her hand from his grasp, she shifted her weight onto her right leg, looking unconvinced. "It's not me that you have to reassure."

The door to the infirmary swung open, and he thanked God in silence for the interruption. But when a familiar red-headed skunk strode across the room in their direction, his pale skin newly painted with splatters of green and yellow, Treyton's thankfulness was consumed by a belly full of repulsion.

His fingers itched, and temptation seeped into his lungs. If he could convince Klara to lend him her pen, he would gladly sign his work.

"Where is she?" Quercus' voice was sharp. Hurried.

Impatient.

Treyton swallowed, defying his brain and its every impulse to jump on the man and batter at his face with his fists.

"She's busy," Klara answered, her eyes wandering toward the restroom. A flash of concern crossed her expression. Miles' minute had been up a while ago.

Treyton might have imagined it, but he could have sworn that the older Arxman was puffing out his chest, sizing them both up. Treyton would have met the challenge if he'd had more muscle in his chest. Most of his strength was in his arms and legs.

"The director would like to meet with her urgently."

"The director can afford to wait another minute or two," Klara replied with a challenge to her modulated tone.

Quercus' jaw tightened. "I can assure you that the director cannot afford to waste such valuable time on the likes of Miles."

Heat surged to the tips of Treyton's ears. The guy showed up out of the blue after years of disappearance, and suddenly he and the director were buddies?

He stepped toward the older man, ready to decorate the other half of his face with his fist, when he noticed Klara's disapproving glare out of the corner of his eye. If he retaliated, his actions would only support her suspicions about him and his peculiar relationship with Miles.

Though the resistance went against everything that was natural to him, Treyton held a hand out to Quercus as his way of "apologizing" for their earlier skirmish.

Quercus glared at his hand, as though he had just licked it in front of him. "Call her out."

Assface.

As hard as Treyton was fighting to nurse his composure, even Klara's patience was wavering—the usual glow in her cheeks was reddening. And not because she found Quercus charming.

"This is my infirmary, Major Salices. I appreciate your loyalty to your job outside those doors"—she pointed to the entrance with an uncertain finger—"but here, you're under *my* command. Do I make myself clear?"

Treyton couldn't fight the smile that crept across his face.

Take that Querc-ass.

Quercus gave a curt nod. "Very well."

The door to the restroom creaked open, and out walked Miles. She moved awkwardly in her new attire, still gripping at the black fabric that clung to her skin. In fact, she was so distracted, making adjustments to the uniform, that she failed to notice Quercus' added presence in the room until she had nearly stumbled into him. Treyton reached out a hand to steady her.

Miles gave a start when her eyes caught Quercus', and she stepped back to stand next to Klara, the women's shoulders brushing. Rather than moving away to give the Ascendant woman room, Klara leaned into her as though to reassure her.

"The director would like to meet you," Quercus said, levelling his gaze at Miles. Like a jaguar stalking its prey, moving with precision, one paw after the other.

Ready to spring.

TWENTY

MILES

A scream tore its way up into my throat, catching on the breath that I was holding. There, it made a home for itself. Embedded itself into my flesh like a parasite, feasting on my fear. The memory of his hands restraining my arms where the tips of his fingers had burrowed against my flesh lingered, kick-starting my heart into overdrive. I grew lightheaded at the roaring of my blood through my veins.

Swaying back, I widened my stance, trying to keep upright. But every breath threatened to topple me over. How was it that someone who had once brought me so much comfort—who had at one point in our lives made me feel the safest—repulsed me now? Like two south poles of a magnet, repelling each other, projecting us further from one another.

The man that stood before me wasn't the Quercus that I remembered. The man standing before me was Quercus' vessel, possessed by the mind of a man I'd never met.

Quercus cleared his throat. "The director would like to meet you, and I'm afraid that we won't be taking no for an answer."

He was observing me with his large, green eyes, which were murky with grey flecks. In our youth, I'd found them calming. Serene, even. But now they carried the ferocity of barbed vines, daring to wrap around my ankles and pull me into the dark cavern of his mind.

To break my skin, drawing seething beads of my blood.

"The director?" Though my voice was no more than a whisper, the word was harsh against my tongue.

Unnatural.

Yet another reminder of how foreign their world was to me.

"She's the founder of the Resiliens," Klara explained, her shoulder still pressed against mine. "She's aloof, and she lives and breaths within the confines of her office. I've never even met her."

That's reassuring…

Swallowing against the lump of intimidation forming in my throat, I decided to lock my attention on Klara and Klara alone. If I looked Quercus in the eye, my voice would evaporate into nothing. Meanwhile, Silens' attention was already occupied, his eyes severe and aimed at Quercus.

A chill raked its way down the length of my arms. Even in his earlier outburst, Silens hadn't seemed an angry person. The behaviour hadn't suited his smooth face and pink lips, which were so often parted by a white-toothed grin.

Now, he looked more like his brother. His eyebrows were furrowed together, a line drawn between them. A vein rippled the skin of his forehead. If I stared at it long enough, I could see it pulsate.

I hesitated, trying to think of a response. "She sounds…nice."

In reality, though, she didn't sound nice. She seemed important, with indispensable time. And if she was requesting me specifically, sacrificing that time just to speak to me, the nature of our meeting must be of incredible importance.

I brought my hand to my collarbone, massaging the base of my throat and drinking in a long breath. "Did she mention why she wants to see me?"

Despite my better judgement, I searched Quercus' face for an answer, avoiding his eyes and focusing more on the scars on his face—white streams parting the rough, flesh-coloured land on either side. I might have imagined it, but I could have sworn that I saw the hardness in his face disturbed by a brief quiver of softness. But when I blinked, it disappeared.

"I'm not at liberty to say," was all Quercus replied, turning his shoulder toward the exit.

I swallowed hard. Whether I liked it or not, I'd have to follow him. I couldn't just defy him—he was strong enough to throw me over his shoulder and carry me there himself. And the sliver of my dignity that remained was already chipping at the edges. There was no way it could sustain another blow.

Nodding to display my compliance, I started to follow him across the infirmary, holding my hand up in farewell to Silens and Klara as I went. But before I'd made it four steps toward the infirmary doors, a hand gripped my wrist.

Stiffening, I yanked my arm toward me and turned to find Silens, whose hand had fallen to hang limp at his side. His icy eyes were slick with apology.

"I'll come with you," he said. There was something to his tone. Like if he spoke too loud, the noise might fracture me.

Before I could stop myself, the word fell from my mouth: "No."

Obviously expecting me to be grateful for the offer, Silens hiked up an eyebrow. "No?"

This time, more certain than before, I answered, "I'll be okay."

Silens' demeanor shifted.

"Go get 'em, tiger," he said, curling back his lips to offer a smile. Returning it with a small grin of my own—a response as unnatural to the muscles in my face as it would be to a man like Murus—I hurried after Quercus, who waited in the doorway, eyes like bullets tearing through my skeleton and obliterating my insides.

Any flicker of pride I'd had in standing up for myself died out as I fell into step next to him, the silence, thick as molasses on an autumn's eve, suffocating. Conscious of how close he was to me, only an arm's length away, I bit the inside of my cheek.

We turned left out of the infirmary and paraded down the long stretch of tunnel in front of us. Dull blue lights illuminated the walls, making the trip seem more eerie than it already was.

There wasn't much to view, or admire, in the tunnels. Every wall was made of the same stone, lit by the same shade of light. There wasn't so much as a single work of art to liven up the walls, the stone interrupted only by the steel slabs for doors that indicated the existence of other rooms or sectors.

An underground prison.

What began as one tunnel branched out into four, and we continued down the second from the left. The further we went, straying further and further from the others, the more my nerves buzzed. The path we followed branched out twice more before something in the air changed. A cool breeze caressed my skin, planting kisses along the lengths of my arms.

My coat, slung over the spine of a chair, was back in the infirmary. Glancing down at myself, I blinked, having forgotten about the thin, black uniform I was dressed in. At first it had bothered me, but as time passed it had become a second skin, assuming the shape of my body. Each step was freeing without the burden of the weight of my regular Ascendant attire, which had hung loose against my small frame and earned some drag when I moved.

The broad-shouldered man brought his hand up to shield his gaping mouth as he broke out into a yawn. Peering up at him from the corner of my eye, I allowed my mind to wander.

Last time I'd seen him, he'd been forceful. Insistent. But now he

ignored me, looking at me no more than once every few minutes to ensure that I was still following. And he was quiet, too. We'd been walking for what must have been twenty minutes, yet neither of us had muttered a single word. Though there was nothing particularly boring about the circumstances, or the fact that my entire schema about the world had been flipped onto its back, I couldn't ignore the gnaw of boredom against my skull.

"How much longer?" I asked.

He gave a forced sigh. "There's no need for conversation, Miss Amissa."

Sting.

I tucked a curl of hair that had strayed from my ponytail, which tickled my cheek, back behind my ear. "I was just asking a question."

"Not long," he answered.

I waited to see if he would further contribute to the not-so-necessary conversation, but he didn't. And to my surprise, I was disappointed. As different as both of us were from the days of our unsuspecting bond, his was the only familiar face around. And now that we were alone, it was easy to pretend he'd never vanished at all. That he'd never abandoned me, leaving me to defend myself, knowing full well that I was incapable of surviving without him. If I concentrated, I could picture him as the boy I'd loved all those years ago.

"It isn't far now," he said finally, sensing my disappointment.

"Have you ever met the director?" I asked.

"Of course."

Intrigue perched itself atop my head, weighing down my mind. "What's she like?"

With a flash of amusement across his face, his resemblance to his eighteen-year-old self was uncanny. My nerves steadied themselves, no longer on high alert.

"She's a lot like you," he answered, turning his head to look

down at me.

I nodded, unsure as to whether or not I should be flattered or horrified. If she was anything like me, she was weak. Another woman without a voice. But something told me that wasn't quite the case. The Resiliens weren't the Ascendancy, after all. Women here were entrusted with power and knowledge. Both things I'd never had the privilege of knowing, not even with my own advantage as a daughter adopted into a highly respected line of men who had devoted themselves to strategic eugenics. Some, however, would argue that women being deprived of power was systemic oppression.

"You grew out your hair," Quercus commented, the words no louder than a whisper.

Reaching up to run my hand over my ponytail, I nodded. "Mr. Koura kept insisting I cut it all the way up to my ears."

A laugh erupted from Quercus, catching me by surprise. "Your dad must have loved that."

I flinched, the blood in my veins icing over. The mere mention of my dad sent a sharp pang piercing through my heart like an arrow laced with acid. Another reminder that life had changed for me after Quercus had left, after he'd forgotten me. Forgotten about my dad's death.

"He's dead."

Quercus stopped in his tracks, his freckled face whitening.

"Miles…"

I shook my head violently. I didn't want his pity. It was ten years too late for it.

"Was he sick?"

If he'd stayed, he would've learned the truth. He could've helped me process the grief that I'd been forced to suppress for too long and had to contain even now. But he hadn't, and he had the nerve now to ask questions.

"Depression," I said with a clipped tone, unable to meet the intensity of his gaze. I didn't want to see the green in his eyes dim or his lower lip twitch as it did when he was concerned. I didn't want to see him at all, if I was being honest with myself. It had been silly of me to think that if he'd stayed, things could have been different. Even if he hadn't left, nothing would have changed. Murus would still be the cruel man he was, and my dad would still be dead.

But at least I would have had someone.

For the remainder of the trip, both of us were quiet. I was muted by the tension constricting my airway. Whatever it was that had been bridging the gap between us gave way to the forces of gravity, splintering into scraps as it plummeted into the end of the universe.

I'd underestimated both the complexity and length of the tunnels. The entrance had been just tall enough that I could have skipped down the steps without skimming the ceiling with the top of my head. But underneath the surface of the planet, the ceiling stretched sixteen feet up, the width of the tunnels enough to fit handfuls of people should they stand shoulder to shoulder.

The further we went, the more branches we encountered—the more secrets there were to uncover and pathways to follow. There was a whole world down here, containing a society of its own. I made a mental note to ask Klara later if they had constructed any sort of map so that I could familiarize myself with their base, since it seemed I would be staying a while.

We came to a stop outside a door made of the same steel as the rest. This door in particular, though, had a golden doorplate with one word etched into it in bold, black lettering: *DIRECTOR*.

TWENTY ONE

MILES

UERCUS RAPPED ON THE DOOR, warning the person on the other side of our arrival. He then nudged it open with his shoulder and closed it behind us as I stepped in after him.

We walked further into the heart of the room. It was smaller than I'd imagined. A dark, wooden desk was pushed up against one corner, leaving no room for much else. Yet, even with the space being as small as it was, I failed to notice the figure sitting in a chair in the corner opposite us until they rose to their feet, turning to face us.

It was a woman, and she was holding something rectangular in her hand. Wooden. In the center was a printed image—a photograph? But before I could get a good look at it, the woman placed it facedown on her desk.

She moved to greet Quercus, her long black coat sweeping the floor around her ankles, and pulled him into a tight hug. Now that she was closer, I could see that sewn into the collar of her coat was gold thread, forming lettering in a language I did not recognize. It was the same lettering that had been carved into the chairs in the

room from yesterday.

When the older woman pulled out of the hug, I averted my gaze, not wanting to call attention to my curiosity.

"Miles."

Her voice was silvery, and she spoke my name as though we were old friends reuniting after years of reluctant separation.

The irony was enough to make my lip quiver, threatening a grin, as I stole a glance at Quercus. But his focus was elsewhere—on the photograph concealed from our eyes.

"Hi," I said. A greeting seemed like the only appropriate response. "It's a pleasure to meet you."

A smile broke out across the woman's lips, brightening the room. It was infectious, much like Silens'. Before I had the chance to fend off the temptation, I parted my lips into a small sliver of a grin in return.

I'd done more smiling today than I'd done in a decade.

Now that the woman stood only a couple of feet from us, I took the opportunity to study her face. It was the only way to read a person without verbal discussion.

Though she had a youthful glow about her, the lines seeping out around her eyes betrayed her age. *She's old enough to be somebody's mother,* I thought. Did she have a wife? Kids of her own? Or had she dedicated her life to the Resiliens, with no time for personal aspirations and desires? Perhaps she balanced both, and her family was located somewhere within these tunnels, unaware of our meeting.

"I apologize for how cramped it is in here, but I thought you might appreciate somewhere more private."

I nodded, folding my hands in front of me. "It's quaint."

Quercus cleared his throat, blowing out his cheeks. "I'm sorry to interrupt, Director," he said, bowing his head. "But it's time I take off. Alessandra will be here any moment to accompany you both."

I bit the inside of my cheek. He was going to leave us alone? Together?

The director nodded her head with a sunny frown. "Next time don't wait so long to come and visit me, would you?"

Quercus didn't reply, only flashed a smile. Then, without so much as looking my way, he excused himself from the room, shutting the door behind him.

"You're conflicted."

The director smoothed back her long, black hair, which was ticked with grey, gathering it in her hands before releasing it into a river of soot sweeping down the length of her back.

I kept still, pressing my lips together. I was conflicted, but I wasn't going to admit that outright. At least not to her, no more than a stranger.

"You don't have to tell me," the director continued, as though reading my thoughts. "I can tell just by looking at you. You've got your father's eyes."

You've got your father's eyes. I repeated the words in my head, over and over.

My chest tightened and the floor began to sway underneath me, the surrounding walls swinging toward me. Squeezing my eyes shut, I braced myself, tensing my muscles.

I waited for the cement to close in around me and juice the life from my fragile body. My ears strained, listening for the splintering of my bones or the *pop* of my internal organs as they exploded under the immense pressure.

When I opened my eyes, the walls and floor were still again. But every breath was a roar in my ears. My vision was fuzzy as I swept the room with my gaze. The director's voice, calling my name, was distant, no more than a purr in the air, drowned out by the thunder in my chest.

A hand squeezing my shoulder tethered me to reality again, an anchor against the world in my head; a reflection of my memory. Everything was the same—Murus, my dad's death. Yet my fears were amplified.

Paralyzing.

Just yesterday I had belonged to the Ascendancy.

To Murus.

And yet that way of life was as unfamiliar to me as the life I was living as I stood before the director, who was bending her lips into a concerned frown as I continued to ignore her calls.

I was wandering the territory of the in-between, which was populated by no more than myself and the unknown. The unidentifiable. And I was making my way aimlessly, searching for a sign. For a connection. Something, *anything* to make sense of it all. Of myself. Of the world as it crumbled around me. Anything to point me in the right direction.

Life within the Ascendancy had meant certainty. No one had to make the important, influential decisions, because they'd been made for us, predetermined before we were even born. In the Ascendancy, there was no guilt. No regret. No wanting to turn around and go back. No wondering how things could be different. The Ascendancy only moved forward.

And if you so much as turned your head, they would destroy you before you had the chance to scream.

Under the Ascendancy, there was no anticipation. You would wake up one morning and carry about your day as normal, unaware that that particular day was significant in that it might be your last. And by the time you knew that you were breathing your last breath, strapped down to a metal table, an IV tapped into your veins, it was over. Your daughter's last encounter with you—her last memory of your face—was presented to her by a monitor, hours after your death. And there was no moving backward.

I squeezed my eyes shut, trying to draw any semblance of the

memory of my dad's face to the front of my mind. When it wouldn't come, my jaw tightened.

Murus had taken him from me.

He'd been gone before I'd even gotten out of bed that morning. A six-year-old girl needed her father—a source of trust, reliability, *love*—and Murus had robbed me of that.

My anger bubbled to the surface, consuming my anxieties on the way up. My head buzzed, moisture—sweat—gathering on the nape of my neck. Murus had taken and kept *everything* from me.

My voice.

My dad.

My identity.

Even the truth behind the Ascendancy's ways.

If Murus had trusted me at all…Put any faith in me…

I shivered at the thought. If I'd been born a man, my position might have been different. If I'd been his loyal servant, just as desperate for the sweetness of power upon my tongue as he was…

For the first time in my life, I was grateful that I'd been born a woman.

"There is something that you should know."

I lifted my eyes, guiding my attention back to the director and the world existing within that room.

"Sit down," the director ordered, gesturing to the chair in the corner with long, scarred fingers.

Ungluing my feet from the floor, I did as I was told and lowered myself into the seat with care.

The air in the room had changed. It was heavy, pressing against my shoulders. I held myself still, worried that if I shifted too much in my chair, the repetitive motion would betray my sudden unease.

The director sat against the edge of her desk, folding her hands in her lap. Rather than at me, she stared up at the ceiling. Her face contorted, and I tilted my head.

She's in pain.

"Listen to me," the director said, her voice brittle, as though evading tears. "What I'm about to tell you should in no way affect the way you view the Resiliens or anybody here."

Her voice trailed off.

I bit the inside of my lip, leaning forward in my seat. What could be so important—or rather, horrible, given the way she was acting—that the director, who had seemed so level-headed and resilient until Quercus had dismissed himself, was grappling with the words trapped in her mouth?

The director cleared her throat, wiping away a tear that had escaped and was forming a wet trail over her cheek.

"Are you all right?" I asked, unwilling to keep sitting there without acknowledging her suffering.

The older woman nodded, resting her forehead in her hands and shutting her eyes.

"I thought I would know what to say when—*if*—this day came.…I rehearsed the words over and over again in my mind every day for years, so sure that I would know how to do this. But now that you're here…"

Another tear escaped, following its sister's path.

I turned my head and looked away. To continue to watch her cry would be an invasion of her privacy. I understood better than anyone that tears were an object of vulnerability.

Murus frowned upon crying. When I was young, after my dad had passed, he would strike me if I dared to cry.

"Crying is a woman's job," he would say.

It had only been when I grew older that I recognized Murus' inability to outgrow his denial about me being a girl. And it raised the question—which I still couldn't answer—of why Murus, already a wealthy and notable figure amongst the Ascendancy even at a young age, had agreed to adopt a girl, knowing that I could never

earn respect or build upon the family name.

The director rose to her feet. My gaze followed her as she made her way to the door and, as though she were about to leave, reached for the doorknob. Her fingers lingered against the metal knob. Now her own feet seemed to be glued to the floor.

Over her shoulder, in a ghost of a whisper, she uttered something that I almost failed to catch.

Almost.

"I'm your mother."

TWENTY TWO

CURRENS

A FAMILIAR PAIR OF EYES, a mixture of mottled brown and green hues, bored into his face. They were wet, trembling from side to side as they darted around the black canvas of his subconscious.

They were searching for something.

Anything.

A way out, or answers—he couldn't be certain.

Currens reached out a hand, offering it to them, though unsure of what exactly he could offer. There was no cure for the expiration of life.

The eyes crept closer, their edges darkening and the face they belonged to revealing itself to him.

Rupedo.

The young boy's face wore a subtle frown. But the longer Currens held his gaze, the more the frown stretched until his lips were like razors against his face, carving bloodied lines horizontally across the hollows of his cheeks. Droplets of blood trailed down his glowing skin, lingering on the edge of his chin, as though clinging to life,

before succumbing to gravity's reign and falling into the dark.

The ruin.

The nothing.

Currens tried to steady his voice. "Rupedo, your face." But the boy didn't hear him, or didn't want to. The gashes stretched further back, the skin on the sides of his face sagging into two gory yawns. Pink trails stained his tanned skin.

Jerking into an upright position, Currens balled the sheets in his fists, the fall and rise of his chest in rhythm with his heart as it slammed against his ribcage. At first, he had a hard time deciphering where he was. The room was small and dark, in no way like his own. But as the fogginess of sleep departed, his memory returned to him, including how he'd ended up here in a room he recognized to be one of the many on-duty rooms that Arxmen utilized in between long patrols or general shifts.

Kicking off the covers that had gotten tangled around his ankles in his sleep, he retrieved his wristwatch from off the bedside table, pulling it tight around his wrist and securing the buckle. As he placed his bare feet flat against the ground—he'd left his shoes by the door—the muscles in his leg were shaky. Fatigued. He frowned as he tried to recall the last thing he'd eaten, but came up short. With the Res Novae upon them, thrusting every Resiliens Arxman into high gear, as well as the Amissa girl's arrival setting every civilian on edge, he was lucky if he got a wink of sleep these days.

The day before, he'd worked a sixteen-hour residential patrol. It wasn't until his patrol mates had urged him to get some rest that he'd retired to the on-duty room, using his remaining strength to kick off his shoes and collapse into the bed, still wearing his uniform from the day before.

Unable to read the hands of his watch in such a poorly lit room, he reached for his shoes and exited out into the tunnels, easing the door shut behind him. As he bent down, slipping each shoe onto its

respective foot, the anthene morphing to the shape of his feet, he caught a glimpse of the time: 1300.

Had he read that incorrectly? He blinked his eyes, thinking that sleep still clouded his gaze, and his chest tightened when nothing changed. It still read the same. He was nearly an hour late.

"Irrumabo."

"Well, thank you for taking your time," Tata hissed through clenched teeth as Currens entered the room, easing the door shut behind him.

He bowed his head. "My apologies, Father," he said, his words broken by heavy pants. He had come from the residential sector on the north end of the base, running in an effort to shorten what was normally a thirty-minute trip on foot to the military sector in the south end, where the conference room was.

The muscles in his legs groaned, and by now, the fatigue had spread to his arms.

When Currens lowered himself into a seat at the foot of the table, being careful not to move so quickly as to send his head reeling, Pater rose from his seat at the head of the table and moved to sit in the chair closest to him.

"Have you been taking care of yourself?" he asked, lowering his voice as though intending to keep his words private. But there was no need. The three of them knew the state of Currens' condition, leaving nothing to be kept secret.

Currens nodded, hoping to brush the subject off. There were other issues at hand, and his own personal health was the least of his concerns. Especially now that there was work to be done.

"As the head of civilian security, I worry that we are not doing enough," Currens began.

Pater seemed to be caught off guard by the sudden change in

priority and drew his eyebrows together. "There are patrols around the clock, Currens," he said. "We can't ask our men to work any more than they already are."

"So we increase the sizes of our patrols."

Tata shook his head. "That would be ridiculous. People are already exhausted as it is working the shifts we have in place now. And there aren't even half enough people to do the work that you are proposing. We don't have the manpower."

"The civilians are getting antsy," Currens argued. "More fights have broken out in the past month and a half than they have over three years. We need to do more."

Throwing himself back against the spine of his chair, Tata pinched the bridge of his nose and breathed out a long sigh. "We don't need more security."

"The news of Miss Amissa's arrival has spread throughout the residential sector," said Currens. "People are startled, confused. They want answers, but until we can provide them with any, they will just continue to retaliate against any form of control. If we do not have enough—"

"Oh, for God's sake, Currens," Tata interrupted. "*No.*"

Pater shot a look to Tata, who, though he made his displeasure clear with a grunt, submitted to silence.

"What your father means to say is that fear is a natural response to this sort of thing. Fear is what makes us human. It's what sets us apart from the Ascendancy. Unless the fighting poses a substantial threat to the safety of our civilians as a whole, we need to allow them to be afraid. Uncomfortable, even."

A surge of annoyance swelled in Currens' chest, an annoyance that he could only repress by curling his hands into fists so tight that his nails left white half-moons in his palms. Something was wrong, and here they were turning a blind eye.

That was the trouble with the art of survival. When it meant

deciding between fighting or fleeing, there was an instant in time where you were stuck. Frozen. And in that very instant, you needed to reorder your priorities and realize what needed immediate attention—what you could afford to sacrifice.

The sacrifice his fathers were making, and at what cost, he wasn't yet sure.

Civilians were becoming resistant. The night before, two men had gotten into a fistfight in the west end of the residential sector, disturbing everyone from their sleep. And the cause for their tussle had been trivial—in walking opposing directions, one man had misstepped, shouldering into the other.

By the time Currens had arrived, the fight had escalated into a flurry of swinging blows, bruises, and merciless words.

How much longer would his parents try to shield the other civilians from the true nature of the threat that loomed over those very tunnels? Civilians no longer knew who to trust but understood that a war was lurking in the shadows, consuming the anxieties that emitted from them in waves powered by enough force to knock a grown man out from under his own feet.

The squeal of wood scraping against cement reverberated throughout the room as Tata thrust his chair back, rising to his feet with a glint to his eyes. "I'm dismissing this meeting until further notice," he said. Though Currens might have been imagining it, the words seemed to be pointed his way.

"Tata," Pater started, but fell silent under the clearing of someone's throat.

The three men's heads turned collectively, the tension that had been accumulating between them split by an added presence in the room. Leaning against the entrance, Major Salices had his arms folded across his chest. He was wearing a smirk plainly on his face.

Currens cleared his throat. He hadn't even heard the older man come in.

"Major Salices," Pater said, regarding the other Arxman with a tepid look. "May we help you?"

"I just heard the commotion from outside. Everything all right?"

Moving around the side of the table, Tata inched closer toward Major Salices, who still lingered near the doorway. His eyes were cold and stern, his lips pursed together and his chin tucked in toward his chest. "I do not take kindly to eavesdroppers."

The ball of Major Salices' throat bobbed as he swallowed, tucking his own chin closer to his chest under the scrutiny of Currens' father.

The two eyed each other for a moment longer before Pater came up behind his husband and entwined his fingers in his, opposing Tata's intensity with a reassuring grin. "We were just leaving."

A weight piled onto Currens' chest, and the floor swung out from under his feet. Before he could stumble, he caught the spine of a chair and lowered himself into it. Arching forward, he rested his elbows on his knees and drank in slow, deep breaths, keeping his face low in order to not draw attention to himself.

After his parents and Major Salices had exchanged their wired goodbyes, the steel doors squealed shut, indicating Currens' solitude. He ran a hand through his ruffled hair, aware that he hadn't had much time when he'd woken up to make himself decent. Nor to take his insulin, which was beginning to take a toll on his body.

"Someone looks rough."

Currens gave a start in his chair, unaware that Major Salices had remained in the room. He grit his teeth, trying to hide his annoyance. What kind of respectable person, never mind an Arxman, lingered in a room in silence without making their presence known? Not only was it peculiar behaviour, but it was an invasion of one's privacy. He remained silent, curious as to why Major Salices was there.

"Word on the street is that you're your parents' right-hand man," he said, striding across the room. His broad shoulders and knowing smirk exuded confidence as he clambered up onto the conference table to sit cross-legged in front of Currens.

"What are you doing, Major Salices?" he asked, narrowing his eyes at the other man's boots. Their bottoms were encrusted with dried mud, which crumbled off and sprinkled over the table's surface. He tried not to wrinkle his nose.

"Please, call me Quercus," he insisted. "Major Salices is too formal. I'd prefer to get to know you...casually."

"Casually?" Currens inquired, hiking a brow.

Major Salices leaned forward, bringing their noses inches from one another. The major's breath, both warm and gentle, grazed against Currens' face.

As the major buried a hand in his pants pocket, riffling around for something, Currens stiffened. He locked eyes with the older man, whose bottom lip curled inward and tucked under his incisors. He was grinning, Currens realized before the stiffness in his body alleviated.

The major pulled his hand from his pocket to reveal a granola bar. "Have you eaten yet today?"

Currens narrowed his eyes at the oat bar, which was fused together by sugar and syrup. In his current state, with his insulin levels as low as they were, consuming that amount of sugar would send him into diabetic ketoacidosis—which could very likely kill him.

"Yes," he lied, diverting his eyes.

Major Salices shrugged, as if to say, "Your loss," before splitting the wrapper and taking a bite of the breakfast snack. Only after he'd swallowed the mouthful did he speak again.

"So what were all the dramatics about just then?"

"Pardon?"

The major's eyes gained a glint as he scrutinized Currens' face as though trying to solve the puzzle behind his eyes. "From what I overheard, you were making a pretty reasonable proposal."

Currens lifted his chin. "What is it you want to hear from me, Major Salices?"

The red-haired man threw his head back in laughter, his pointed canines gleaming under the light. "I think I know what your problem is."

Heat surged in Currens' chest. His annoyance was making a revival. "I don't have time for your antics. *You're* my problem."

Major Salices snickered. "Damn straight, I'm your problem," he said, leaning in close again. Currens could smell the sweetness on his breath now.

"If you ask me," the major said, "I'd say that the Venuses don't value your opinion as much as everybody seems to think."

"Then I suppose it is a good thing I didn't ask," Currens muttered.

"So Daddy's boy does have a spine after all." Quercus rested his chin in his hand, regarding him with his kelly-green eyes. "If I were you and my parents treated me like a child rather than their peer, I'd be rethinking my loyalties."

"Wise words, coming from someone who betrayed his own father," Currens said, recalling the other man's own Ascendant origins.

"Point: Venus." Quercus took another bite of his bar, chewing slowly. "But you and I are more alike than you think, my friend."

Currens couldn't help but crack a grin at that. What had given him that suggestion? They were merely strangers. Acquaintances by coincidence, perhaps, but certainly not any closer than that. In fact, Currens had made a point of not making friends. Those he worked alongside were his peers, and those he worked to protect—civilians—remained distant. From his perspective, personal relationships only hindered performance.

"You're quite confident about knowing who I am," he said.

The major began to pick at his teeth, trying to remove an oat that had lodged itself in his gum line. Currens wrinkled his lip and tried

not to stare too hard at the other man.

"Well," Major Salices began, wiping his hand, and his saliva, on his pants. "I'm no more confident than you are determined to drive me away."

"I beg your pardon?"

"Beg received, and pardon granted," the major answered, setting his half-eaten granola bar down on the conference table and leaning toward Currens again. "Now quit changing the subject. What's up with your parents?"

Currens grit his teeth. His hands gripped his thighs, and his fingers curled into the material of his uniform pants. "What are you insinuating?"

"Like I said, they don't seem to value your opinion. Why is that?"

"And they must not value you as a member of their staff, given that I had no idea who you were until yesterday. Why is *that*?" Currens countered, fed up with the other Arxman's adamant prodding.

The major gave a self-deprecating laugh and raked his fingers through his shaggy copper hair.

Though the older man had laughed before and he had paid it no mind, Currens found something intoxicating about his laugh now. Before, it had been sharp and abrupt. But in that moment, it was soft and drunken.

"I can't say I'm not disappointed," Major Salices said, holding Currens' gaze. "I had hoped you'd notice me, given our current chemistry."

A wave of heat lapped at the apples of Currens' cheeks and seeped into his chest. He opened his mouth to respond, searching for the right remark. Yet he only stumbled over his words. It was as if his tongue had swollen up to three times its size and was now squirming against the roof of his mouth.

The major's lips cracked into a thin, childlike smile. It was almost cocky, in an innocent sort of way. "I know I noticed you."

Currens turned his face away and all but leapt out of his seat, itching to put distance between him and the other Arxman. *Why is he being so…direct?*

The major picked up his granola bar again, took a bite, and chewed. Currens watched as his jaw flexed a moment before he caught himself ogling and cleared his throat.

"There is a reason the director put my parents in charge of leading the Resiliens," Currens answered. "They know best."

Major Salices nodded slowly. "I have a proposition for you."

Currens raised a brow and shot him a questioning look.

"Let's take a walk."

TWENTY THREE

SILENS

THE LIEUTENANT GENERAL HAD JUST FINISHED tying the laces of her work boots when Treyton inched open the doors to her quarters, which she frequently left unlocked in the event that her security services were needed. Still careful to respect her boundaries, both physically and personally, he lingered in the doorway, shouldering against the door's frame.

"Is something the matter, Venus?" Alessandra asked, retrieving her phone and various other items, which she ordinarily carried on her person, from off her bedside table.

If he wasn't going to get any insider information about his fathers' future plans from Klara, unearthing it from the depths of Alessandra's brain wasn't going to be any easier a chore. With Klara, he had tried the approach of voicing his suspicions about his family. This time, he would have to level with her and make their secrecy a matter of civilian security.

"What do you know about phase two?" he asked outright.

Alessandra, clearly caught off guard by the abruptness of his questioning, blinked at him. "Repeat that?"

"Phase two of the Res Novae. What's involved?"

She gave a small shake of her head. "I will not be the one to disclose that information to you. Take it up with your supervisors if you have concerns."

Treyton suppressed an amused huff. He'd already tried that approach many times, and they'd only ever turned a deaf ear in his direction. If only he wore James' face and held his ranking. Maybe then someone would take him seriously.

"My supervisors have their priorities elsewhere. Besides, I figured that my concerns were in your field of interest."

"How so?" Alessandra straightened up, putting a pause to her shuffling around the room to train her attention on him. Her brow creased, and Treyton knew that whatever he said next would make or break his chances of collecting any new information.

"I worry that they plan to weaponize the Amissa girl," he admitted, puffing out his chest somewhat in a display of confidence.

Whichever way the lieutenant general's thoughts were wandering, she didn't let her expression give it away. She stood as stoic as a redwood tree unrelenting to nature's pummeling forces. "What makes you say that?"

"When they introduced her profile, they said that her disappearance would provoke a reaction out of the Ascendancy. But from everything we've learned about her in her time here, Murus Amissa wouldn't risk anything to ensure her well-being."

The words left a stinging taste in his mouth. Only in a world that the Ascendancy had dictated would a parent discard their child only because of their sex. Still, Treyton thought there was something peculiar about Miles' existence altogether. Miles' being a girl could have come as no surprise to her parents, seeing as Ascendant couples were able to reject adoption profiles paired to them through the Ascendant government, and yet Murus had adopted her anyway. But for what reason? Just to torment her and use her as his emotional plaything? Treyton's skin squirmed.

"And?" Alessandra said.

"The Resiliens' beliefs have always existed on a foundation of rationality and of violence as a last resort. But Miles Amissa has a fifth-tier ability, making her the most powerful, and possibly dangerous, inhuman on the planet. They could be using her 'relationship' with Murus as a cover to prevent Resiliens civilians from revolting at the idea of a war."

"My God," Alessandra mumbled, her words hardly more audible than a whisper. "You're serious, aren't you?"

Treyton hesitated, and his heart fluttered for a moment. What kind of question was that? "We're up against the Ascendancy. We're bound to lose, unless by a means of immeasurable force. *Inhuman* force."

A flash of something brightened the lieutenant general's eyes. Treyton clenched his jaw, half expecting a tsunami of heat to wash over him, but was flooded only by relief when the sensation remained dormant. At least for now.

"I'll tell you one thing," Alessandra answered, keeping her voice low enough that anyone passing by out in the hallway wouldn't be able to listen in. "But you didn't hear it from me." Her words were sharp. Threatening.

Treyton, more aware of the sound of footsteps bouncing between the cement tunnel walls than before, shut the door after him and drew a few footsteps closer. A silent agreement.

"The Resiliens are a sizable underground movement," she began, crossing her arms. "But our military forces are only a fraction of the Ascendancy's, making an all-out war impossible to win."

Despite his acquired taste for the vigour of combat, Treyton nodded his agreement. When he had made his oath to defend the Resiliens as an Arxman, as every twelve-year-old who was eligible and willing to defend their cause did, he'd understood that the odds were not in their favour; that he'd essentially signed away his life in committing to the vows he now recited annually.

"The Ascendancy retains power through intimation and force," said Treyton. "We can't match up."

Alessandra uttered a sigh. "Even if we manage to weed out the Ascendant government, there will be men after us who will rise to the occasion. The Ascendancy is more than just a council of men governing mankind. It's an ideology. The only way to dismantle the ideology is to dismantle their beliefs."

A chill raked the back of Treyton's neck. In other words, they needed to reveal the Ascendancy for what it really was and hope to God its citizens' faith in humanity would be enough.

But what did that mean for Miles?

"So we give them something else to believe in?" he asked.

"We give them a god," Alessandra answered, resolve in her voice.

Now it made sense. His parents didn't plan to use Miles as a weapon at all. Rather, they hoped that her power would strike fear into the heart of the Ascendancy and rewire its entire frame of thinking.

A religious transmutation.

"You should prepare yourself," she said, disturbing his thoughts.

"Prepare myself?"

"Because if we fail, the Resiliens will fall. Forever."

"And so will all of us," Treyton responded.

Alessandra nodded her head solemnly.

TWENTY FOUR

CURRENS

After accepting Major Salices' offer to take a walk, Currens had been surprised to find out that the proposal hadn't been one of personal intent. Rather, the invitation had been to join Major Salices' evening patrol, above ground and out of Currens' jurisdiction.

The patrol consisted of the major, himself, and two other Arxmen: one woman, who was twice his age, with riverbeds of experience etched into her ageing face, and a man who Currens estimated was about Major Salices' age. They were expected to trail alongside the Resiliens' borderline. Ascendant patrols had been venturing nearer to the line with each passing day. Their job was to keep a low profile and report their findings back to the lieutenant general without provoking any Ascendant officers or initiating unnecessary, and potentially lethal, contact.

The four of them were now hugging the southwestern side of the border. The other two Arxmen ventured strides ahead. Currens was sure to keep close to Major Salices, who seemed to be in no hurry as he dawdled after the other half of their group.

Currens cast a sidelong glance at the flame-haired man. He wondered why he had been invited at all. Patrols of this manner were outside his skill set, and he was unlikely to make any further contributions. If anything, he posed a risk. His being there made their group larger, increasing the risk of detection should their paths cross with those of an Ascendant patrol.

"Rosa, Acinus," Major Salices called out. The other Arxmen halted in their tracks and threw looks of concern over their shoulders. "Move further west," he ordered. "Ascendant officers may be keeping watch from afar. But don't venture too far in case I need to call you back."

For a moment, the older woman, who Currens assumed to be Rosa, seemed to hesitate. He thought that she might be about to argue with her superior when her head snapped back around. Without a word, the two adjusted their course, progressing westward until they were only silhouettes out in the grassy plains.

Despite finding it peculiar that Major Salices would want to separate the group, Currens remained quiet. It wasn't his patrol to lead, after all, and he had to trust his peer's professional judgement.

"You look puzzled," Major Salices said, kicking a loose pebble along with the toe of his boot as they strode forward.

"Not at all," Currens responded. It was a harmless enough lie. He had his concerns, but they weren't sound enough to accuse Major Salices of any ill will.

The pebble hit the edge of the toe of his boot as they fell into stride with one another, sending the stone askew into a patch of tall, yellowing grass.

"I meant what I said about getting to know you," he said. "I figured now was as good a time as any."

Currens wrinkled his nose. "You're on duty, Major Salices. Now is not an appropriate time at all."

The major chuckled. "Let me tell you a story. If you still have no interest in getting to know me personally, I'll comply with maintaining a strictly professional relationship. Deal?"

The early-afternoon sun bathed Currens' skin in warmth as he turned his face toward the sky and shut his eyelids against the yellow light. "Fine."

"Like you," Major Salices began, "I was born under the Ascendancy. I was content with my life there, too, until my father inserted me into the Resiliens' system."

Currens' eyes widened at that. His father, General Salices? As in *the* General Salices of the Ascendancy? His reaction must have been apparent, as the major gave a short, stifled laugh.

"When I turned twelve, like many young Arxmen, I underwent my first undercover mission. But things went awry, and my comrades were killed. It was only because of my father that I was forced to remain undercover amongst the Ascendancy for an additional six years."

To Currens' surprise, Major Salices stopped short in his tracks to stand in place. As he turned to face him, Currens toed at the dirt with his boot, forming a basin in the earth where rainwater would collect after the next early-autumn shower before seeping into the dry earth below.

Though he was listening, he couldn't find it in himself to maintain eye contact. The story was far more personal than he had anticipated, despite not being unlike his own. They had both been forced to change their way of life on the basis of their survival.

"He took me under his wing and made me an Ascendant citizen again. But after those six years, my father believed that I was in too much danger to return to either of my lives. I couldn't remain in the Ascendancy, but I also couldn't return to the Resiliens until the time was right. I know people have their suspicions about me. But *that* is why nobody is familiar with me."

"How long?" asked Currens.

Major Salices hesitated. "Pardon?"

"How long were you in hiding?" he clarified.

"I was on the brink of my eighteenth year," Major Salices answered. His voice sounded brittle, as though it might splinter into shards if he spoke too loudly. "Ten years."

A forbidding chill sank its teeth into the back of Currens' neck at the thought of ten years of isolation. Ten years of walking the line of the unidentifiable, neither ally nor foe. When his own fathers had fled the Ascendancy, risking their lives to ensure his own, Currens' identity had been determined for him. And since, he had remained loyal to that identity. Not because he was loyal to the man that it made him, but because he was loyal to the men that it made his parents. He owed them that much, even if it meant depriving himself of choice.

"I'm sorry," Currens said.

Major Salices leaned in toward him as though about to say something into his ear. His voice dropped to a whisper, the breath of his words velvety against Currens' cheek. "Told you we had something in common."

Goosebumps raised along the length of Currens' arms as he turned his face away from the other Arxman, eager to conceal his reddening cheeks from his keen-eyed peer.

The corners of the major's pink lips twitched, betraying his amusement. He then started onward again, dragging the heels of his boots ever so slightly over tussocks of yellowing grass as he walked. Currens followed.

The eerie snap of a twig from several feet away made Currens jump in his shoes. The major sucked in a breath, as though afraid that if he exhaled too forcefully, it would draw the attention of whatever, or whoever, was nearby.

Major Salices bent his knees, lowering himself gradually closer to the ground. With no tree cover to shield them from sight, getting as close to the earth as possible was their best chance at avoiding detection. The major tugged at Currens' pant leg, using his eyes to instruct him to follow his lead.

As Currens did as he was expected to and crouched, he misstepped, and his balance dwindled. He swayed toward the other Arxman, who shot out an arm, snaking it around his waist to steady him.

Currens' heart beat hard against the inside of his chest. The major's hand was warm against his bare midriff where his shirt had ridden up. The skin-to-skin contact was enough to send him reeling.

"Shouldn't you call back the others?" Now that he had regained his balance, Currens straightened his spine and shifted away from the other man's touch.

"They're too far away. Calling them might only draw unwanted attention." The major pressed a finger over his lips, gesturing for him to stay quiet, before getting onto all fours and pressing his belly against the ground. Currens thought to follow him as he snaked his way forward, making diligent movements, but decided against it.

Major Salices' red hair was a stark contrast to the pale yellow of the grass, as was his dark Resiliens uniform. In the past, Currens had been glad for the open landscape that stretched toward the horizon as far as the eye could perceive. But in that second, he had never more yearned for a canopy of green to protect them.

"Over there," the major said in a low voice.

Following his gaze, Currens' stomach twisted into a knot. Three Ascendant officers were off in the distance, standing between them and the other half of their patrol. They had spotted the other Arxmen and were headed straight for them.

"Irrumabo," Currens cursed, jumping to his feet before the major could reach out to stop him. He broke out into a sprint toward the rest of their group. The older Arxman called out after him, but his attention was trained solely on their separated comrades. He

wouldn't let them fall prey to the same fate that Emere had. He couldn't.

The grass whipped at his calves as he ran, pumping his arms to propel himself forward. The craggy western mountains reached skyward, toward the early afternoon sun. Their peaks were sharp, threatening to skewer the pregnant gray clouds above, which scattered about the sky as though startled apart like a flock of fleeing sheep.

"Halt!" one of the officers called, but Currens turned a deaf ear to the warning as he continued to close the stretch of land between him and the others. The other two officers had detained Rosa and Acinus. While Acinus hung his head and seemed to be complying with his arrest, Rosa was tossing her head back, trying to nail the officer holding her arms behind her.

Currens had made it within thirty feet of the others when something grabbed hold of his wrist, jerking him backward.

"What the *fuck* were you thinking?" the major spat, spraying saliva as he raised his voice. "You just blew our cover, Venus."

Chest rising and falling rapidly as his lungs heaved, Currens stared down at Major Salices' lingering fingers in disbelief. "We can't just stand here," he hissed, yanking his arm away.

The major opened his mouth to argue, his crystalline eyes hot with indignation, but was interrupted by several cracks of a gun. They both spun on their heels, eyes wide in the direction of the officers. Acinus was struggling now against the officer that held him, his sobs and the red splatter freckling the yellow grass both signifiers of foul play.

Rosa's still form was slumped over the arm of one of the officers.

Currens had failed. Again.

"No. No, no, no." Currens' knees buckled underneath him, unable to resist gravity's pull.

An arm swept the air in front of him before curling around his waist and pulling him close. He tilted his face upward to look into the major's regretful face, and the world around him began to shift. A lightheadedness took hold of him as the edges of his vision blurred. The yellow grass around them seemed to swim in circular motions, and the mountain peaks smeared the light blue sky with gray.

"Currens, can you hear me?" Major Salices gave the side of his face a few light slaps with his free hand, his other arm still snug against Currens' torso.

Currens nodded. With what energy he had remaining, he lifted his left arm and shook his sleeve until it slid down to his elbow, revealing a silver medical bracelet. He had always made sure to keep it hidden from plain view except in the case of an emergency.

Major Salices stiffened as he peered at the bracelet's engraving. "Hell, Venus." The words were light, like a thin breath of air. "Did you take your insulin today?"

Shaking his head, Currens' dizziness only worsened. Although he knew that the Ascendant officers were growing nearer by the minute, their voices sounded far off in the distance. He swore inwardly, cursing himself for neglecting his health for as long as he had, putting them both in jeopardy now.

"We've got to get you out of here," the major said, swivelling him in the direction that they had come.

"Acinus," Currens breathed. Major Salices shot him a soft but stern look.

"There are three officers and one of myself, Currens. His fate is sealed."

Currens was about to object when the major's arm slipped out from around his waist. He stumbled forward, barely catching himself, both hands laid flat against the ground, fingers splayed. "What the—" he started, but when he glanced up to glare at the older Arxman, two officers had a hold of him, each clutching an arm.

A surge of adrenaline pounded through Currens' veins. Those

arms had readily held him upright. He remembered the warmth of the major's hand against his skin and his breath billowing against his cheek. His eyes narrowed at the officer's hands on him, and a searing heat flooded his chest.

Slipping his blade from its sheath, Currens forced himself upright. The officers had dismissed his presence due to his condition; their attention did not waver from their current target.

If they were to make it back to base unharmed, or at the very least alive, he needed to ensure the major's freedom.

"Ascendant scum," he called out, his voice slicing the tension that polluted the dry, musky air. He waved his blade above his head. A challenge.

To Currens' surprise, there was a flicker of panic in Major Salices' eyes. One of the officers bent his arm behind the major's back, instructing his partner to hold him steady before advancing on Currens.

The officer broke out into a sprint toward him, his hand travelling to his waist and retrieving a knife similar to Currens' own. This weapon, however, was larger in length, and the blade curved inward at the tip. Currens grimaced as he imagined the hook embedding itself into his skin before being torn out; he could hear the ripping of flesh in his mind, smell the reek of blood lingering in his nostrils.

Currens leapt out of the way as the officer swung his blade toward his face. Tightening his grip on his knife, Currens jabbed it toward the officer's lower back. Before the knife could graze the officer's white uniform, the officer seized Currens' arm, leaving him open.

He tried to pry the officer's arm off, but his grip was too tight. The officer thrust his blade at Currens' chest, but, to both their shocks, the blade only bent against the surface of Currens' shirt as though the weapon had been made of paper.

"You're one of them," the officer breathed, his voice trembling.

Startling back, the officer dropped the mangled blade, leering at him with his mouth agape. "Inhuman filth."

The accusation filled Currens with dread. "You're mistaken," he said, unsure as to why he was arguing with a man who would soon be dead.

"Your kind are unnatural."

His own circumstances aside, Currens was reminded of those that he, like his brother, had sworn an oath to protect. His job right now was to return his peers to safety, and not to reinforce his identity to those who intentionally turned a blind eye to the truth of the inhuman.

"If you want my *kind* dead, you're doing a poor job of it," Currens taunted, widening his stance and tightening his grip on the hilt of his dagger. The officer read into the challenge, raising his crumpled weapon in return.

Currens bounded forward, slicing the air in front of the officer's nose. The officer ducked, thrusting his weapon at Currens' legs. The blade was soft as a feather as it swept over his kneecaps; the fabric of his pants split by the blade's demand, but his skin underneath resisted the sharp metal.

Kicking his leg out, Currens planted his foot square in the centre of the officer's chest, propelling him backward. The officer fell onto his back with a *thud*, the air knocked from his lungs as his white form squirmed over his bed of yellow.

Currens towered over his opponent, his dagger an extension of his arm. He gripped a handful of the officer's long, dark hair in his free hand, yanking it upward so that the officer was forced to look him in the eye.

"I would sooner die in the name of the Ascendancy than I would mingle with the likes of you, savage," the officer spat.

"So be it."

Currens jabbed his blade into the side of the officer's neck where

the carotid artery ran and watched as the gloom of death seeped into the officer's gaze, smothering what was left of his light as his brain was deprived of oxygen.

"Currens!" the major shouted, his voice straining. The other officer had him pinned to the ground with a hand against his throat.

Releasing the dead officer's hair and letting the corpse fall, Currens threw himself over Major Salices' attacker. Just as he had wrapped his arms around the officer's throat, forcing him into a hold, the bellow of a gun roared in his ears.

Major Salices' cry split the air, which sent shards of panic through Currens' heart. The memory of Emere's pain-filled wailing rang in his ears; the air surrounding them seemed to thin, making it harder for him to breathe. His head spun. His arms quivered, still swaddling the officer's neck.

An elbow met Currens' face, sending him reeling off of the officer. Falling flat on his rear, he gaped at the Ascendant man who had the gun still in-hand.

"Time for you to join your friend," the officer hissed, his lips twisting into a cruel smile. He lifted his weapon, leveling it at Currens, who sucked in a breath and prepared to submit to his fate.

Before the officer could fire his gun, however, the major was on his feet again, shouldering against the officer.

The gun fell to the ground and out of the officer's reach. Currens, too, returned to his feet and charged forward, blade in his grasp. He toppled the officer off his feet, pinning him down as he had done earlier to Major Salices. In a flurry of rage, Currens stabbed the officer with his dagger once and then twice. And then again. And again. Again.

Again.

Again, even after the officer's body had fallen still.

Blood splattered his hands and his face. It speckled his dark uniform. The dark droplets shimmered like starlight where they sat in the grass like dew under the sun's rays.

It wasn't until he heard a gentle moan that he stopped mutilating the officer's deceased form and looked up. Major Salices was crumpled over the grass, almost completely still. If it weren't for the faint rise and fall of his chest, like a wave of air rolling over the plains after sunset, Currens might have thought he was dead.

Replacing his dagger into its sheath, Currens hurried over to his injured peer. He lifted the major's head into his lap and ran a hand over his forehead and ruddy hair in a slow, soothing manner. Blood moistened Major Salices' uniform around his right shoulder, where the bullet had taken refuge in the Arxman's body.

"Major Salices," Currens said, careful to keep his voice low. The major, however, failed to respond.

Currens waited another moment before placing a hand on the major's cheek, lowering his head so that he could hear his whisper, if at all. "Salices?"

Tears rimmed Currens' eyes. An ache, different from anything he'd ever felt, radiated in his chest.

Loss.

He had lost lives before, and yet this was the first time he was really, truly experiencing it. When Emere had died under his supervision, he had experienced failure. Guilt. But this loss that he was facing, knowing that the major may never stir awake, was unlike any cut or scrape or bruise he'd endured the pain of before.

"For the love of all that is good on this planet, call me Quercus, would you?"

The major's eyelids fluttered open to reveal his jade-green gaze that, despite everything, was glittery with amusement.

EPILOGUE

QUERCUS

"THEY KNOW."

The silence that hung after those two words coiled tighter around his neck.

"About?" the voice on the other end of the call answered, pressing for more information. The voice was rough, like it belonged to someone who had made a habit of swallowing gravel. Quercus, even from hundreds of miles away, could see his thorny black stare and his curled lip in the back of his mind.

"About her ability."

There was a rustle of movement on the other end of the line, followed by a *humph*. "Spit it out, Officer Salices." Judging by the added sharpness to his tone, he was growing impatient.

"Not anything specific, but they're getting closer. They'll be running tests. It's only a matter of time before they figure it out and find a way to use her against us. Whatever her ability is, they know it's powerful. There have only been two people ever known to have a fifth-tier ability. Her, and your—"

"That's enough," the voice on the other end interrupted.

"Sir?"

"They've evacuated, haven't they?"

"They're relocating the ill and the injured first, sir."

Shuffling sounded again from the other end of the call.

Is somebody in the room with him?

Quercus swallowed, trying to focus his attention on the doorway. If anyone were to walk in and overhear his private conversation, the harshness of the voice on the other end of the line would be the least of his problems.

"Listen, I don't have much time," he said. "Tell me what you want to know, and tell me how you're getting me out of this mess."

"Do I sense my apprentice getting grumpy?"

Quercus grit his teeth, swallowing a remark that crawled to the tip of his tongue and dangled off the end like a leaf in the wind. "Not at all, sir."

"Good. Now, why don't you tell me where your little friends are hiding?"

"They're not my—"

"*Ahem.*"

"They're heading north, toward the mountains," he answered.

Quercus thought he saw a blur of movement out of the corner of his eye. His every nerve seemed to explode in his body as he pressed the burner phone to his chest, eyes pointed at the vacant space in the doorway. Whatever it was he'd thought he'd seen, it was gone now—if it had existed at all and wasn't just a product of his own bubbling paranoia.

"Officer Salices? Officer Quercus Salices, are you there?"

Quercus, hearing his boss shouting at an increasing volume through the phone, brought the device back to his ear. He lowered his voice when he answered, in case someone happened to be lurking outside the room with their ear to the wall. "I'm here."

"Where are you now?"

"A bunker. A small group of us—the sick and the injured, like I said—stopped here to rest for a few hours. It's a four-hour trip north of their base."

His hand travelled to his bandaged shoulder, where the white polyethylene was soaked through with his own blood. The bunker was poorly stocked with medical supplies, much to his surprise. He would have thought that they'd have made an effort to be well prepared, should their plans to demolish the Ascendant government go awry.

As they would.

"You're injured?" There was an air of surprise to his boss' voice.

"Just a little nick. Nothing I can't handle, sir."

"Very well. I'm dispatching a unit out there now, so I suggest that you get your ass in gear unless you want to be dead with the rest of them."

Buds of panic were beginning to bloom in his chest. Each beat was stronger and more painful than the last. Any harder and he feared that his heart would burst.

The image of Currens' weary face flashed in his mind. His sunken eyes, and his skin, blotchy with emotion after Quercus had taken a beating in their fray with his fellow Ascendant officers. Had it not been for Currens, he would have died at the hands of his allies, his efforts to the Ascendancy repaid by a cruel twist of fate.

"Quercus?"

He stiffened. His boss hadn't addressed him by his given name since he was eighteen, only months before he had been sent away. When they spoke over the phone, he addressed him only by his Ascendant-declared ranking, followed by his surname. Salices. His father, and his grandfather before him, had worked diligently to do well by their family name. A Salices man was an honourable man, according to his father. Excitement tugged his lip into a small grin as he imagined his father's horrified face when he discovered that his

own son was working against him, leading the Ascendant army into a war already set to be won on their behalf.

"Yes, sir?"

"You're a good boy. Loyal. You've never tried to steer me wrong. If only you'd been my child all along, all of this could have gone more smoothly."

"Sir?"

"Before you hang up, I have one more favour to ask of you."

"Your wish is my command," Quercus answered.

"My daughter has proven to be a thorn in my side. I need you to get rid of her."

Get rid of her? Did he mean…?

"Get rid of her how, exactly?" he asked.

Murus grunted. "Do you seriously need me to spell it out for you, Officer?"

That was all the clarification he needed. The request, though ambiguous, was clear to him. "No, sir," he said. "It'll get done."

"Good boy. I'll make a king of you yet."

Without so much as a farewell, Quercus ended the call, letting the phone fall against his lap as he gawked at the wall in front of him. Though he wasn't sure how as of yet, Miles Amissa would be dead well before the sun had passed the zenith.

TO BE CONTINUED...

ACKNOWLEDGEMENTS

When I'd tell people that I was a writer as a kid, they would ask if I ever planned to publish anything. The answer was always no. When you are ten years old, writing stories from the perspective of animals, you can't imagine that you'll one day come to publish anything. If only I'd been kinder to myself, maybe I could have published this book sooner. On the other hand, this book came into existence at a time of transformation in my life. If I'd done it any sooner, I can't say it would be the same book that I've come to love.

Thank you, Mom and Dad (Nerm!!!), for nourishing my love of books at an early age.

To the Toronto Public Library, for supplying my unrelenting appetite for fictional worlds and blue-eyed love interests.

To Bradyn, for steering me right. If it weren't for the discussion we had that late night on the couch about what I *really* wanted out of life, this book might still be a fraction of a first draft. And as much as I'm sure you grew tired of hearing me ramble on about countless plot points and fictional characters, I appreciate every second you (reluctantly) listened. I couldn't ask for a more supportive brother.

To John. There were times when I wanted to give up. Thank you for not letting me, and for being my cheerleader. You were excited when I couldn't be.

To Ella and Karo, for being two of my literary guinea pigs.

Without your enthusiasm, I might never have finished the second draft.

To my lovely beta readers—Allison, Applez, Ayesha, Gabriel, Logan, @artistic.arcana, Salma, Shay, and Stelle. When I sent out the first manuscript, I was so nervous to have someone aside from myself read my book for the first time. Your comments and constructive criticism were incredibly helpful. I appreciate every single one of you.

To Emma from Emerald Ink Publishing for making me a better writer and for restoring my enthusiasm toward this novel. As nervous as I was to work with an editor for the first time, you were incredibly supportive and encouraging. I adore you!

And finally to you, the reader. Thank you for not only purchasing my book, but for reading it. I hoped you enjoyed it as much as I enjoyed creating this world and these characters that I have come to love so dearly. They say that an author should never get too attached to their characters....My bad.

ABOUT THE AUTHOR

KIARA J. MCKENZIE is a Canadian author who writes dystopian and fantasy fiction. *Central Line* is her debut novel. She often incorporates her high school love of biology (more specifically, the allure of genetics) with her first love, storytelling. Kiara is a loyal family member and friend. When not staring at a computer monitor for several hours a day, whether because of school or writing, she can be found spending quality time with those she loves.

She is currently a full-time student at the University of Toronto. Specializing in English, she is working toward her Honours B.A. After university, Kiara would like to expand her knowledge and explore copy-editing courses.

Connect with Kiara on Instagram: @kiaramckenzieauthor

CPSIA information can be obtained
at www.ICGtesting.com
Printed in the USA
LVHW091146241120
672481LV00020B/1927

9 781777 194703